RABINDRANATH TAGORE

BROKEN NEST
& OTHER STORIES

TRANSLATED BY
SHARMISTHA MOHANTY

ekadā

ekadā

First published by Tranquebar, an imprint of westland ltd, in 2008

Published by Ekada, an imprint of Westland Books, a division of Nasadiya Technologies Private Limited, in 2025

No. 269/2B, First Floor, 'Irai Arul', Vimalraj Street, Nethaji Nagar, Alapakkam Main Road, Maduravoyal, Chennai 600095

Westland, the Westland logo, Ekada and the Ekada logo are the trademarks of Nasadiya Technologies Private Limited, or its affiliates.

ISBN: 9789360459376

10 9 8 7 6 5 4 3 2

Typeset by Mukul

Printed at Manipal Technologies Limited, Manipal

BROKEN NEST

& OTHER STORIES

Rabindranath Tagore (1861–1941)—poet, playwright, novelist, painter and composer—reshaped Bengali literature and music in the late nineteenth and early twentieth centuries. Of Tagore's prose, his short stories are perhaps most highly regarded: he is credited with originating the Bengali-language version of the genre. He was awarded the Nobel Prize in Literature in 1913.

Sharmistha Mohanty is the author of three works of prose, *Book One*, *New Life* and *Five Movements in Praise*, and two books of poems, *The Gods Came Afterwards* and *Extinctions*. She is the founder editor of *Almost Island*, an online literary journal.

Contents

Foreword

I have been reading the stories of Rabindranath since my youth. These four are certainly among them. I have felt drawn towards these stories, as if in kinship, like many other readers in Bengal. In each of these works, the fiction writer Rabindranath's strength manifests itself in its fullest measure. A very long time has passed since these stories were written, many extraordinary works have been created by writers of later times—even then the radiance of these stories has not dimmed, instead they have become even more luminous with time.

A long time after the writing of these stories, they have been translated into English by Sharmistha Mohanty. She is a contemporary writer. She was born more than a century after Rabindranath. Before I began to read these translations there was an apprehension working in my mind. How will I feel when I read them? It is not the aim of a translation to merely tell the story. The aim is to be able to grasp Rabindranath's prose. What is more, the language in each of these four works is different. I had reservations.

When I finished reading, I was amazed. Sharmistha has been able to render both the rhythm of the prose, and its essence. And the language that it has been translated into has also retained its spontaneity and ease. Secondly, there was a fear that the inner substance of these stories would get lost in translation, at least in some places. But Sharmistha's main achievement is here—she has not allowed any erosion of that inner substance. This is possible because Sharmistha has grown up experiencing Rabindranath's language.

When we read a work in translation, very often we see that the translator is attempting to remain always alert and faithful to the original. This attitude is a necessary one. But an excessive alertness of this kind often represses our experience of the original—without the translator's knowledge. The desire to be faithful to the original and its consequent responsibility often leaves the translator no room for her own experience of the work and her own response to it. This experience, this response, is necessary. Not because the translator should have the freedom to move away from the original. But because she must experience the writing through her own being. If she can do that then she will be able to touch its essence and spirit.

Sharmistha Mohanty has experienced these writings very deeply, from her own place. On the one hand reading these translations one can touch the ease and flow of the original language, on the other hand its spirit remains intact. This is hard work. It needs effort. But this hard work has not left its imprint on these pages. This work is far from self-conscious. In this translation, Rabindranath is found through his stories. This is a very significant thing.

—**Joy Goswami**
Translated from the Bengali

Preface

If there is one thing that flows like blood through the veins of these stories, it is helplessness. Their power is in the endurance and strength that lies after it. Tagore's direct narrative prose is clear water. At times the light changes over it, a shadow passes, and when night falls the water too takes on night's opacity. The reasons for power and pain cannot always be traced to their precise sources.

Charu can do nothing as the man she loves goes away, to a place she can never reach, like Ratan, the little girl whose employer goes back to the city, leaving her behind, and Uma, powerless as her only notebook is taken away from her. This is a woman's helplessness, a woman in a certain place and time, but like any phenomenon seen keenly, it becomes more than itself, becomes a complex aspect of the human.

I use the word helpless, and no other can be substituted for it. That is what these women are, because there is no hope that anything will be redeemed in their lives. 'Amal is in good health, yet he does not write. How did this complete and terrible break come about? Charu wants to ask Amal this question and receive an answer, face to face, but there is an ocean in between and no way to cross it. Cruel separation, helpless separation, beyond all questions, beyond all redress, separation.'

The only thing for them to do is endure, and this they are infinitely capable of. There is a significant presence of water in these stories, that predominant element in the Bengal landscape. But it is always the men who move, over rivers, across seas, and the women must allow everything to pass over and through them, shadows and brutality, sudden stars and indifference.

The profound connection, perhaps even an equivalence, between movement and human freedom is fundamental. The women must always be in stasis, because they can never leave, or return to their parents' home or go with the one they love. There is Ratan falling at the postmaster's feet, and the postmaster moving away from her on the river, Charu clutching the four poster bed as her husband leaves her behind in an empty house, Uma falling to the floor after having to give up her notebook and 'clasping the earth in a tighter embrace'.

Since they cannot run, they can only stand or fall to the ground, either way to be earthed, while movement surrounds them, uncontrollably.

This stasis is really the final and greatest suffering. In movement so much can be forgotten, left behind, made lighter. As the postmaster's boat begins its journey he thinks he should go back and get Ratan, 'but the sails had caught the wind, the monsoon current was flowing swiftly, the village had been left behind and the cremation ghats could be seen on the riverbank—and in the wistful heart of the traveller being borne away on the river there arose this philosophy, there are so many separations in life, so many deaths, what is the point of returning?'

In the brief paragraphs or lines where Tagore's prose approaches the attitude of poetry, he brings one closer to the centre of the story's consciousness. This can happen anywhere within the work, but it always happens once again at the end, where he separates the contexts of movement and stasis as if for ever.

These are women of unbearable dignity, forced into a suffering to which they are almost always equal, and the only travelling they do is towards an acceptance of that stasis within which they must live. They do not have a helpless attitude towards helplessness, neither do they try to overcome it by trying to break whatever holds them back. Their greatness of spirit lies in the way they face their suffering and still continue to give.

'The Ghat's Tale', written in 1884, was Tagore's first short story, and the earliest in the language. Writing over a hundred years ago, entering the lives of women across class and caste, across urban and rural contexts, Tagore's understanding goes much further than compassion.

In a culture and a time where marriage and family were seen as the fulfilment of a life's expectations, these stories shatter the complacence of those beliefs.

As Tagore makes his initial relationship with the form of the short story, the work is direct and as loosely held together as a tale being told to a listener. Authorial interventions and digressions recur.

Over the years, of course, his art in the medium of fiction grows complex. In these stories the growth is in how he steps further into his characters, into their inner spaces. 'Broken Nest', the latest of the works collected here, is one of his greatest works of fiction. The other element which has evolved is Tagore's mastery over what cannot be said. 'Broken Nest' is an unusual achievement. The novella makes certain things manifest, but in a way that the recognition of these things does not need to be articulated. It is a reminder, strangely enough, of our tradition of the 'akatha katha', the narration of that which cannot be narrated, what is unutterable, unspeakable, unmentionable. This is a profound instance of a culture's way of living that transforms itself into craft.

Bengali and English are vastly different languages, coming from vastly different cultures. If I have chosen to retain the long, winding sentences, the syntax, and the movement of the Bengali, as far as I can, I have done it to remain true to the centre of Tagore's work, and to enable his voice in this other language. This sometimes makes the English a little difficult in places, takes away perhaps a certain smoothness. But any serious attempt at translation bends the host language somewhat, makes it go against itself. The goal of a translation should not be an attempt to make something that reads as if it were written in English. Instead, the translation should retain the dynamism of an encounter.

Essayist and translator Eliot Weinberger, who has been the principal translator of Mexican poet Octavio Paz, and has brought other major writers from Spanish into English, has said, '... the primary task of a translator is not to get the dictionary meanings right—which is the easiest part—but rather to invent a new music for the text in the translation language, *one that is mandated by the original*.'[1] (italics mine)

This risk, if it is one, can also be taken because English is in many ways now an Indian language, and this English is capacious enough to accept certain Indian tones and ways of construction. What Raja Rao had said in the foreword to his novel *Kanthapura*, in 1937, holds as true today. 'We are all instinctively bilingual, many of us writing in our own language and in English. We cannot write like the English. We should not. We cannot write only as Indians. We have grown to look at the large world as part of us.'

Compound words are common in Bengali and these words are very often multidimensional. A word like 'phalparinamhin', for example, has a poetry within itself that cannot be translated. The dynamism comes from the yoking together of

1 Anonymous sources, in *Oranges and Peanuts for Sale* (New Directions, 2009).

two words—fruit and without consequence—to form a new word, where each unit brings its own meaning and emotion. The English equivalent has to be a series of words.

Another difficulty is of course one of culture. The original contains many references to religious, social and philosophical traditions. The word 'bisharjan', that Tagore uses to describe what Bhupati does with his newspaper, has a certain force because of its cultural associations, the immersing of a deity into the river after its worship is over. Another example is the succinct adjective 'abhagini'. It contains a woman's whole life, and nothing in English comes close to its shattering force, its nearest meaning in English, 'a woman abandoned by fate'.

Tagore also changes tenses, within a paragraph, and sometimes even within a single sentence. I have retained his way in most places, so that this sense of time which is special not only to Bengali but to most Indian languages carries through into the English. This coming together of tenses is of course much more than a way of sentence construction, it is a way of being that is embedded within the language.

There is moreover the challenge of translating certain ideas or emotions, one foremost example being the word 'abhimaan'. This translates as a feeling of hurt which a person does not directly acknowledge, and it occurs only in a relationship of great intimacy and tenderness, between lovers, parents and children, or very close friends. There is no equivalent term in English.

Civilisations not only pass down gestures differently, but at times even certain nuances of emotion that impel them.

For a Bengali Tagore is an overwhelming inheritance. But it is an inheritance one must earn. For a Bengali who is a poet and prose writer in English, educated almost solely in that language, but whose emotional world has its home in both, the relationship with that inheritance is extremely complex. The act of translation, for someone like this, becomes an act of facing a loss with confidence, and an act of retrieval at the same time. Only after will the writer see that these acts have had far-reaching and unpredictable consequences on her own relationship with the English language.

—**Sharmistha Mohanty**

BROKEN NEST

1

Bhupati did not need to work. He had enough money and the country was hot. But he was born under stars that made him a man who must work. This is why he had to start an English language newspaper. After that he did not have to lament the endlessness of time on his hands.

Ever since childhood he had liked writing and giving speeches in English. Even when there was no need, he would write letters to English language newspapers, and even if he had nothing to express he would always say a word or two at formal gatherings.

To get a wealthy man like Bhupati into their group, political leaders would praise him profusely, and so Bhupati's idea of his own abilities in English had become well-nourished and full.

In the end his lawyer brother-in-law Umapati, defeated in his attempts to set up a practice, told him, 'Bhupati, start an

English language newspaper. You have such exceptional . . .' etc.

Bhupati became enthusiastic. To have a letter published in another's paper could not really be a matter of pride; in his own, an independent pen could freely run its course. He made his brother-in-law an assistant, and at a rather young age he ascended the editor's chair.

At a young age the intoxication of editorship and politics is very strong. There were also enough people to spur Bhupati on.

In this way, while he was engrossed in the paper, his child wife Charulata slowly stepped into her youth. The newspaper editor did not become fully aware of this significant piece of news. The Indian government's border policies were changing rapidly and breaking all barriers of restraint. This was the object of Bhupati's attention.

In the wealthy house Charu had no work to do. Like a flower that never turns to fruit, and so, outside any necessity, remains in bloom, was Charu's life, and to remain in bloom the only work of her endeavourless, endless, days and nights. She lacked nothing.

Taking advantage of such circumstances, the wife indulges her husband excessively, marital life loses all restraint and goes from timely to untimely, from proper to improper. Charulata did not have any such opportunity. To penetrate the screen of the newspaper and claim her husband became extremely difficult for her.

When a relative brought his attention to his young wife and reproached him, Bhupati, for once, took notice of the situation and said, 'That is true, Charu should have a companion, the poor thing has absolutely nothing to do.'

He told his brother-in-law, 'Why don't you bring your wife here—without a woman her age in this house, Charu must be finding it very lonely.'

It was the lack of another woman's company that was the cause of Charu's sorrow, this is what the editor understood. He arranged to have his brother-in-law's wife, Mandakini, brought to the house, and was relieved.

The time when a husband and wife, in the first glow of the birth of love, appear to each other in incomparable beauty and as forever new, that time, that golden radiance of a marital dawn, passed by, unawares, unknown to both of them. Without tasting newness, both became old, familiar and habituated to each other.

Charulata had a natural inclination towards reading and studying, so her days did not become too burdensome for her. She had, through her own efforts, made arrangements to study. Bhupati's cousin Amal was in his third year of college, and Charulata would take his help and do her studies; to gain this favour she had to grant Amal many of his capricious demands. He often had to be given money to eat at a restaurant or to buy a book of English literature. Amal would sometimes invite his friends for a meal, and the arrangements for this were made by Charulata. Bhupati did not make any demands on Charulata, but in exchange for teaching her a little, there was no end to what Amal demanded of her. Charulata would sometimes pretend to be angry about this and protest; but to be necessary to anyone and to bear the troubles born out of affection became essential for her.

Amal said, 'Bouthan, the Raja's son-in-law comes to our college wearing woven slippers made by special hands in the zenana, I just can't bear it—I want a pair of woven slippers, otherwise there is no way I can maintain the dignity of my feet.'

Charu: Really! I should sit and weave slippers for you now. I'll give you the money, go and buy a pair.

Amal: That cannot be.

Charu does not know how to weave slippers and she does not want to admit this to Amal. But that someone should ask her for something, that Amal should ask her for something—in the whole world there is only this person who asks of her and she cannot bear to leave his desires unfulfilled. When Amal was away at college she secretly began learning to weave slippers. At such a time, one evening, Charu invited Amal.

It is summer and arrangements have been made on the roof for Amal's meal. To prevent any dust flying on to the food, the plate is covered by a brass lid. Amal changed his clothes, washed his hands and face, and arrived upstairs.

Amal sat down and opened the lid, on the plate was a new pair of woven wool slippers. Charulata laughed in delight.

After receiving the slippers, Amal's expectations increased even more. Now he needs a silk jacket, a silk handkerchief that must be embroidered with a flowered border, for the large armchair in his living room a decorated covering is essential to prevent oil stains from his hair.

Every time Charulata protests and quarrels, and every time, with great care and affection, she fulfils the fancies of the aesthete Amal. Sometimes Amal asks, 'Bouthan, how much have you done?'

Charulata lies and says, 'Nothing has been done.' Sometimes she says, 'I didn't even remember.'

But Amal does not let her be. Every day he reminds her and makes new demands. Charu, in order to incite all this trouble from the persistent Amal, expresses indifference and so begins a quarrel and then suddenly one day fulfils his wishes and watches his reaction in delight.

In this wealthy family Charu does not have to do anything for anyone else, only Amal does not let her be without making her work. In the effort to meet these small demands her heart lives its true nature and is fulfilled.

If the land that lay inside Bhupati's estates was called a garden, it would be an exaggeration. That garden's main tree was an English hog plum tree.

For the improvement of this piece of land Charu and Amal had formed a committee. Both of them together had, for some days, drawn pictures, drawn plans, and with great enthusiasm imagined a garden on this land.

Amal said, 'Bouthan, in this garden of ours you have to water the trees yourself like the princesses of long ago.'

Charu said, 'And on the western corner we have to make a shed, the baby deer will live there.'

Amal said, 'And a small pond has to be made, in it there will be swans.'

Charu became enthusiastic at this proposal and said, 'And in it we'll plant blue lotuses. I've been wanting to see blue lotuses for a long time.'

Amal said, 'On that pond we'll make a small bridge and at the bank there will be a small boat.'

Charu said, 'Of course, the bank will be made of white marble.'

Amal took a pencil and paper, drew lines, then holding a compass, began to draw a map of the garden with a show of great pride.

Both of them together, every day, rectified and changed what they had imagined and in this way made twenty-five more maps.

When the final map was made they began to draw up an estimate of the expenses. At first their resolve was that Charu would pay for the garden slowly with the allowance she received each month; Bhupati never notices what goes on in the house; when the garden was completed they would invite him there and surprise him; he would think that with the help of Aladdin's lamp a whole garden has been lifted up from Japan and transplanted here.

But even if the estimate is made as low as possible, Charu cannot afford it. Amal then again sat down to change the map. He said, 'Then Bouthan, let's leave out this pond.'

Charu said, 'No, no, we can't leave out this pond, in it will be my blue lotuses.'

Amal said, 'Don't put a tiled roof on your deer shed. Make it a plain and simple thatched roof.'

Charu became extremely angry and said, 'Then I don't need that shed—let it be.'

Clove saplings from Mauritius, sandalwood from Karnataka and cinnamon from Ceylon, instead of these, when Amal mentioned the names of ordinary native trees available in Maniktala, Charu made a face; she said, 'Then I don't need a garden.'

This is not the way to lower an estimate. To restrain the imagination along with the estimate was impossible for Charu, and whatever Amal may say, inside, even he cannot really accept it.

Amal said, 'No. What fun will there be if we tell him? Both of us will build the garden. He can place an order with a Sahib firm and make an Eden Garden—then what will happen to our plans?

Sitting in the shade of the hog plum tree, Charu and Amal were experiencing the pleasure of imagining their impossible desires fulfilled.

Charu's sister-in-law Manda said, 'What are you doing out in the garden so late?'

Charu said, 'We are looking for ripe plums.'

The greedy Manda said, 'If you find some, bring them for me.'

Charu laughed, Amal laughed. The primary joy and pride of all their plans was this, that it was confined to the both of them. Whatever other virtues Manda may have, she doesn't have imagination; how will she savour the taste of these proposals. She is completely outside all the committees of these two civilised people.

The impossible garden's estimate could not be lowered, the imagination refused to be defeated in any way. So, the committee under the plum tree carried on like this for some time. The places in the garden where there would be a pond, the deer shed, the marble bank, Amal marked these with a sign.

Amal had taken a small shovel and was marking out a boundary for the imaginary garden—at this time, Charu, sitting under a tree's shade, said, 'Amal, it would be very nice if you could write.'

Amal asked, 'Why would it be very nice?'

Charu: Then I would make you write a story describing this garden. This pond, this deer shed, this shade beneath the plum tree, everything would be in it—no one but the both of us would understand, it would be such fun. Amal, try and write, you'll surely be able to.

Amal said, 'Alright, if I can write what will you give me?'

Charu said, 'What do you want?'

Amal said, 'I'll draw leaves and creepers on the roof of my mosquito net. You have to embroider it with silk thread.'

Charu said, 'You're excessive about everything. Embroidering the roof of a mosquito net!'

Amal said many words against keeping a mosquito net as inaesthetically as a jail cell. He said that most people in the world did not have a sense of beauty, that ugliness did not hurt them one bit, and this was why embroidering a mosquito net sounded so excessive.

Charu immediately agreed with this and thought, 'The private committee that we form is not a part of those people', and felt happy.

She said, 'Alright, I'll embroider the net. You write.' Amal said mysteriously, 'You think I can't write?'

Charu became extremely enthusiastic and said, 'Then you must have written something, show me.'

Amal: Let it be today, Bouthan.

Charu: No, you have to show it to me today—go and bring your writing.

The excessive eagerness to read his work to Charu had been an impediment for Amal all this time. In case Charu didn't understand, in case she didn't like it, he couldn't rid himself of his diffidence.

Today, bringing his notebook and blushing somewhat, coughing a little, he began to read. Charu leaned against the tree trunk, stretched her legs out on the grass and began to listen.

The subject of the essay was, 'My Notebook'. Amal had written, 'Oh, my white notebook, my imagination has not yet touched you. Like a child's forehead before the divine ordainer of destiny has entered the room of birth, you are pure, you are mysterious. The day I will write the concluding sentence on your last line, on your last page, where is that day today? Your white child pages cannot imagine, even in dreams, that forever-stained-by-ink conclusion—' etc. He had written a lot more.

Charu, sitting under the tree's shade, listened in absolute silence. After Amal finished reading she kept quiet for a few moments and said, 'Who says you can't write?'

That day, under the tree, Amal first tasted the intoxicant that is literature; the girl who served the intoxicant was young, so was the tongue that tasted it, and the afternoon, full of long, falling shadows was becoming mysterious.

Charu said, 'Amal, we have to pick a few plums and take them, otherwise what will we say to Manda?'

They did not have any desire to tell the foolish Manda about their studies and discussions, so they had to pick the plums and take them.

2

THE DESIRE FOR A GARDEN, LIKE SO MANY OF THEIR OTHER desires, lost itself in the limitless arena of their imagination, Charu and Amal didn't even notice.

Now Amal's writing became the primary subject of their talk and discussions. Amal comes and says, 'Bouthan, a really marvellous idea has come to me.'

Charu becomes enthusiastic; she says, 'Come to the northern veranda—Manda will soon come here to make paan.'

Charu goes and sits in a dilapidated cane chair on the Kashmiri veranda and Amal sits on the raised portion beneath the railing and stretches out his legs.

The subject of Amal's writings is very often undefined, to articulate it clearly is difficult. What he said, in his confused way, was impossible for anyone to understand clearly. Amal himself would repeatedly say, 'Bouthan, I can't explain it to you well enough.'

Charu would say, 'No, I've understood quite a bit; you write this, don't delay it.'

She, understanding some of it, not understanding some, imagining much of it, and often made enthusiastic by Amal's passion, would build something in her mind. That was enough to make her happy and she would become restless with eagerness.

Charu would ask that very afternoon, 'How much have you written?'

Amal would say, 'How much can I write in such a short time?'

The next morning, a little restlessly, Charu would ask, 'Well, didn't you write it?'

Amal would say, 'Wait. Let me think a little more.' In anger Charu would say, 'Then go away.'

In the late afternoon, when that anger had grown and deepened and Charu was at the point of stopping all conversation with him, Amal, pretending to take out his handkerchief from his pocket, would reveal a small portion of a written sheet of paper.

Immediately, breaking the silence, Charu would say, 'There! You have written! Trying to fool me! Show it to me!'

Amal would say, 'It's still not finished, I'll write some more then read it to you.'

Charu: No. You have to read it to me right now.

Amal is eager to show it to her right now; but he would not read till he had made Charu plead for a while. After that Amal would sit and arrange the papers in his hand, take a pencil and make corrections in one or two places, all this time Charu's heart, in delight and curiosity, seemed to lean towards those papers like clouds heavy with water.

Whenever Amal wrote a few paragraphs, whatever it was, and however little, he must read it to Charu immediately. The unwritten part, through discussion and imagination, keeps stirring inside both of them.

Till now they had been involved in the building of daydreams, now, beginning to plough the fields of poetry, they both forgot everything else.

One afternoon when Amal returned from college, his pocket seemed heavier than usual. When Amal entered the house Charu had noticed the full pocket through a window in the inner rooms. On other days Amal does not wait to come to the inner rooms after returning; today, with his heavy pocket he entered the drawing room. It did not seem he would come inside for a long time.

Charu came to the edge of the inner rooms and clapped her hands many times, no one heard her. Charu, somewhat angered, sat on the balcony and tried to read a book by Manmatha Dutta.

Manmatha Dutta was a new author. His style was a great deal like Amal's, which is why Amal never praised him; sometimes he would read Dutta's writing to Charu with an unnatural pronunciation and ridicule him—Charu would snatch the book from him and throw it far away in contempt.

Today when she heard Amal's footsteps she raised Manmatha Dutta's *Kalakantha* to her face and began to read with great concentration.

Amal entered the balcony, Charu didn't even notice.

Amal said, 'Bouthan, what are you reading?'

Since there was no reply from Charu, Amal went behind the chair and looked at the book. He said, 'Manmatha Dutta's *Galaganda.*'

Charu said, 'Oh, don't disturb me, let me read.'

Standing behind her Amal began to read in a mocking tone, 'I am a blade of grass, a small blade of grass; oh red, royally attired Ashok tree, I am only a blade of grass. I don't bear flowers, I don't give shade, I cannot raise my head to the sky, the kokil of spring does not make me its home and from there stir the world with its song—even then oh Ashok tree, don't be indifferent to me from your flowered, high branches; I am lying at your feet, even then don't disdain me.'

Amal read this much from the book and then began to parody it. 'I am a bunch of bananas, a bunch of green bananas, oh pumpkin, roof-climbing pumpkin, I am really a bunch of green bananas.'

Charu, because of her restless curiosity, could not remain angry for very long. Laughing and throwing the book aside she said, 'You're very jealous. You don't like anything but your own writing.'

Amal said, 'You're too open-hearted, even a blade of grass you want to swallow.'

Charu: Alright Sir, don't joke—take out whatever is in your pocket.

Amal: Guess what is in it.

After bothering Charu for a long time Amal took out the renowned monthly journal *Sarorohu* from his pocket.

Charu saw that in it Amal's essay 'Notebook' had been published.

Charu saw it and was quiet. Amal had thought his Bouthan would be very happy. But seeing no sign of happiness he said, '*Sarorohu* doesn't publish just any essay.'

Amal was exaggerating a little. Any kind of usable, ordinary writing the editor got he was reluctant to reject. But Amal explained to Charu, the editor was a very exacting man, he selected one essay from a hundred.

Charu heard this and tried to be happy but she couldn't be happy. She tried to see and understand what it was that had hurt her; no justifiable reason emerged.

Amal's writing was both Amal and Charu's property. Amal is the writer and Charu the reader. Its secrecy was its greatest beauty. This writing everyone would read and many would praise, why this was giving Charu so much pain she did not clearly understand.

But the desire to be read cannot be fulfilled by only one reader. Amal began to publish his work. He also received praise.

Once in a while letters arrived from admirers. Amal would show them to his Bouthan. Charu was happy seeing them, and also pained. Now, to make Amal write, there was no need for only her enthusiasm and encouragement. Sometimes Amal even received anonymous letters from women. Charu would tease Amal about them but she was not pleased. Suddenly, the closed door of their own committee was opened by the multitudes of Bengal's readers who now came and stood between them.

One day, in his free time, Bhupati said, 'Charu, I did not know that our Amal could write so well.'

Bhupati's praise made Charu happy. Amal was being supported by Bhupati, but when Bhupati understood that Amal was very different from the others whom he gave shelter to, Charu experienced almost a sense of pride. It was as if she was saying, 'Why I love and care for Amal so much you have all understood after so long; I had realised Amal's worth long ago, Amal is not one who should be disregarded.'

Charu asked, 'Have you read his writing?'

Bhupati said, 'Yes—no, I haven't actually read it. Didn't have time. But our Nishikanta read it and praised it very much. He understands Bengali literature quite well.'

Bhupati should feel a sense of respect towards Amal, this was Charu's deep desire.

3

Umapati was explaining to Bhupati why he should give premiums along with his newspaper. How the premiums would result in profit and not loss Bhupati simply could not understand.

Charu entered the room once and, seeing Umapati, went out. She came back again after walking for a while outside and saw that both were engaged in an argument about accounts. Umapati, seeing Charu's impatience, made an excuse and left. Bhupati turned his attention to the accounts.

Charu entered the room and said, 'I suppose your work is still not finished. Day and night how you busy yourself with that one paper, I wonder.'

Bhupati set his accounts aside and smiled a little. He thought, 'Nowadays I have no time to turn my attention towards Charu, it's very unfair. The poor thing has few ways in which to spend her time.'

Bhupati said, in a voice full of affection, 'Today you don't have your studies to do. Has the teacher run away? Your school has all the reverse rules—the student is waiting with her books, and the teacher is absconding. It seems like Amal doesn't teach you regularly nowadays as he used to.'

Charu said, 'Should Amal waste his time teaching me? Do you think Amal is an ordinary private tutor?'

Bhupati held Charu's waist, and pulling her close he said, 'Is this an ordinary private tutorship? If I could get the chance to teach a Bouthan like you, then—'

Charu: Oh, stop it. It's enough your being a husband, forget about more.

Bhupati, slightly hurt, said, 'Alright. From tomorrow I will definitely teach you. Bring your books, let me see what you study.'

Charu: Enough, you don't have to teach me. For now, will you set aside your newspaper accounts? Tell me if you can now turn your attention to anything else.

Bhupati said, 'Of course I can. Now my attention will turn wherever you want it to.'

Charu: Alright, good, then read this essay of Amal's and see how marvellous it is. The editor has written to Amal that after reading this, Nabogopalbabu has named him Bengal's Ruskin.

Hearing this, somewhat hesitantly, he took the paper. He opened it and saw the name of the essay was 'Ashar's Moon'. For the last two weeks Bhupati had been making important calculations regarding the government's budget; those calculations, like insects, were moving around in all the nooks and crevices of his head—at such a time he was not prepared to read a whole essay in Bengali called 'Ashar's Moon'. Nor was the essay very short.

The essay began like this—Tonight, why is the moon of Ashar hiding among the clouds? As if she has stolen something from heaven, as if she cannot find a place to hide her disgrace. When, in the month of Falgun, there was not even a handful of clouds in the sky, then, before the eyes of the world she showed herself shamelessly in the open sky—and today that lovely smile of hers—like a child's dream, like the memory of a lover, like a long string of pearls around the head of Durga—Bhupati scratched his head and said, 'Quite good. But why me? Do I understand all this poetry?'

Charu hesitantly took away the paper from Bhupati's hands and said, 'Then what do you understand?'

Bhupati said, 'I'm a man of the world. I understand human beings.'

Charu said, 'Don't they write about human beings in a literary work?'

Bhupati: They write incorrectly. Besides, when a human being exists physically, then why should one look for him among thought-up words?

Saying this he held Charulata's chin and said, 'See the way I understand you, but for that do I have to read *Meghnad Badh* or *Kabikankan Chandi* from beginning to end?'

Bhupati was proud of not understanding literature. But even then, without reading Amal's writing properly, inside he had a certain respect for Amal. Bhupati used to think, 'There is nothing to say, yet to incessantly think up all these words, this is something I couldn't have done even if I had beaten my head against the wall. Who knew Amal was so capable of all this?'

Bhupati did not admit to being a connoisseur but he was not miserly where literature was concerned. If a poor writer besieged him, Bhupati would pay for the printing of his work, he would only say specifically, 'It shouldn't be dedicated to me.' All Bengali magazines, significant or insignificant, weeklies and monthlies, all books famous, infamous, readable, unreadable, Bhupati would buy. He used to say, 'Firstly I don't read, over and above that if I don't even buy books I will be committing a sin which I will never be able to even atone for.' It was because he didn't read that he didn't have the slightest grudge towards bad books, that is why books filled up his Bengali library.

Amal used to help Bhupati correct his English proofs; to ask for his help in deciphering the illegible handwriting in a certain article, he entered the room holding a sheaf of papers.

Bhupati smiled and said, 'Amal, on Ashar's moon and the ripe palmyra fruit of Bhadra you can write as much as you like, I don't object to that—I don't want to impinge on anyone's freedom—but why impinge on mine? She won't let me be without my reading them, what kind of tyranny is this from your Bouthan?'

Amal laughed and said, 'That is true, Bouthan—if I knew that you would tyrannise Dada with my writing, I would never have written.'

Amal was angry with Charu for bringing his cherished writing to Bhupati who was averse to literature and so humiliating it, Charu immediately understood this and was pained. To change the subject she said to Bhupati, 'Arrange a marriage for your brother, then you won't have to be tyrannised by his writing.'

Bhupati said, 'Today's boys are not as ignorant as us. All their poetry is in their writing. When it comes to work, they are very practical. Well, you haven't been able to persuade your brother-in-law to get married.'

After Charu left, Bhupati told Amal, 'Amal, I'm involved in all this trouble with the newspaper, Charu has become very alone. She has nothing to do, sometimes she comes to this room and looks in. Tell me, what can I do? You, Amal, if you can keep her engaged in her studies, it would be very good. Sometimes if you translate English poetry and read it to her then it will help her and she will also enjoy it. Charu likes literature.'

Amal said, 'That she does. If Bouthan studies a little more then I believe she could write very well herself.'

Bhupati smiled and said, 'That much I don't hope for, but the good and bad of Bengali writing Charu understands much better than me.'

Amal: She has a good imagination, it is rarely seen in women.

Bhupati: Even in men it is rarely seen, I am proof of that. Alright, if you can mould your Bouthan, I will give you a reward.

Amal: Let me hear what it is you will give me.

Bhupati: I'll find you another one just like Bouthan.

Amal: Again I'll have to begin with her. Will I spend my whole life moulding someone?

The two brothers belonged to this age, they did not refrain from saying anything openly.

4

Amal has gained a certain standing in readership circles.

Before this he was a mere student, now he seems to have a place in important social circles. Sometimes he reads his work at formal public gatherings—editors and messengers of editors come and sit in his room, invite him to lunch and dinner, many requests come to him to participate in gatherings or be a speaker. In Bhupati's home, in the eyes of the servants and relatives, his status has risen greatly.

Mandakini, till now, had never thought him to be anyone special. Amal and Charu's laughter and talk she would disregard as juvenile and make her paan or do housework; herself she thought of as more important than them and more necessary for the household.

Amal's desire for paan was limitless. Making paan was Manda's responsibility, and misuse of it annoyed her. Amal and

Charu would often conspire and steal some paan from Manda's storehouse—it was one among their many amusements. But the robbing and laughter of these two aesthete thieves Manda did not find amusing.

The truth is that a person who lives under another's roof does not look kindly on others who share that shelter. Manda felt somewhat humiliated at having to do whatever little extra housework she had to do for Amal. Because Charu was on Amal's side, Manda never expressed her feelings, but she always tried to slight Amal. If she got an opportunity she even said things about Amal to the servants, they too joined in.

But when Amal came into prominence, Manda too was affected by it. This was no longer the Amal of yesterday. Now his hesitance, his meekness, has disappeared. The right to scorn others now seems to be completely his. Having established himself in the world, the man who can unhesitatingly proclaim himself, the man who has acquired a certain right, that capable man easily attracts a woman's attention. When Manda saw that Amal was receiving respect from all quarters, she too raised her face and looked at the head that Amal now held high. The bright glow of new pride on Amal's young face enchanted Manda; she seemed to see Amal through new eyes.

Now there was no more need to steal paan. Amal's gain of fame meant this loss for Charu; their bond of conspiracy and laughter was broken; paan comes easily now to Amal, there is never any lack of it.

Besides this, the delight they felt in scheming and keeping Manda away from their little committee was also about to be destroyed. It was hard to keep Manda away. That Amal would think Charu was his only friend, the only one who appreciated him, this Manda did not like. So whenever Charu and Amal were together, Manda, under some pretext, came between them, throwing the shadow of an eclipse. Charu found almost no time when Manda was not present, so that she could at least ridicule the change in Manda's behaviour.

It need not be said that this unbidden entrance of Manda was not as annoying for Amal as it was for Charu. A previously averse woman's heart was now turning towards him; he experienced inside himself a certain eager desire for this to happen.

But when Charu saw Manda from far away and said in a sharp, low voice, 'There she comes.' Then Amal would also say, 'So I see, how annoying.' To express intolerance of everyone else's company was a custom with them, how could Amal suddenly give it up? In the end when Manda came near, he would say, as if with a forced courtesy, 'So then, Manda Bouthan, were there any signs of paan theft today?'

Manda: You get it whenever you want, then why steal?

Amal: There is more delight in that than in asking for it and getting it.

Manda: What were you reading? Go on and read. Why did you stop? I like listening.

Before this, Manda had never wanted to be appreciated as a lover of literature, but time works wonders.

Charu doesn't want Amal to read before the unappreciative Manda, Amal wants Manda to hear him.

Charu: Amal has written a criticism of *Kamalakanter Daptar*, will you—

Manda: I may be stupid, but that doesn't mean I don't understand anything when I listen.

Then Amal remembered another day. Charu and Manda were playing cards. He had come in with his writing in his hands. He was impatient to read his work to Charu and seeing that the game was not about to end he became annoyed. In the end he said, 'Alright, Bouthan, you both play, I'll go and read my work to Akhilbabu.'

Charu grabbed Amal's shawl and said, 'Oh, sit down, where are you going?' Saying this she quickly lost the game and so ended it.

Manda said, 'Are you going to start reading? Then I'll go.'

Charu said politely, 'Why, you can also listen.'

Manda: No, I don't understand all that rubbish of yours; I only begin to feel sleepy.

Saying this, and annoyed at both of them for ending the game early, she went away.

The same Manda was today eager to hear a criticism of *Kamalakanter Daptar*. Amal said, 'Good then, Manda Bouthan, you will listen, that is my good fortune.' Saying this, he turned the pages and was about to begin from the beginning again; the opening of the piece was elegantly written and he did not want to leave it out.

Charu quickly said, 'Thakurpo, you had said you would get some old monthly journals from the Jahnabi library.'

Amal: Not today.

Charu: You were supposed to go today. Have you forgotten?

Amal: Why should I forget? You had said—

Charu: Alright, don't go. I'll go and send Paresh to the library.

Charu got up.

Amal feared trouble. Manda understood, and in a few moments her mind became poisoned against Charu. After Charu left and Amal was wondering whether to get up and was hesitating, Manda smiled a little and said, 'Go, make up to her. Charu is angry. If you read to me you will be in trouble.'

After this it was difficult for Amal to get up. Somewhat angered at Charu, Amal said, 'Why? What trouble?' Saying this he spread out his papers and was about to begin reading.

Manda covered the papers with both her hands and said, 'There is no need, don't read it.' Saying this, and as if controlling her tears, she went away.

5

Charu was away on a visit. Manda was sitting in Charu's room braiding her hair. Amal entered the room, saying, 'Bouthan.' Manda knew for certain that Charu's absence was not unknown to Amal. She laughed and said, 'Oh, Amalbabu, who did you come looking for and who did you find. This is your fate.'

Amal said, 'The straw on the left is the same as the straw on the right, the donkey loves both as much.' He sat down.

Amal: Manda Bouthan, tell me stories about the village you come from, I'd like to hear some.

To gather material for his writing Amal listened to everything that everyone said with great curiosity. For this reason, he no longer disregarded Manda like before. Manda's psychology, Manda's history, all were now interesting for him. Where she was born, what her village was like, how she used to spend her childhood, when she was married, all this he asked about in detail. No one had ever expressed so much curiosity about the small and trivial events that were Manda's life. Manda, in great joy, began talking about herself; sometimes saying, 'I don't even know what I'm talking about.'

Amal encouraged her and said, 'No, I like it, carry on.'

Manda's father had a one-eyed rent collector, he would often have a fight with his second wife and vow to fast. In the end, overcome by hunger, he would come to Manda's house and eat secretly. Suddenly one day he was caught by his wife. When Manda was telling this part of the story, and Amal was listening in great concentration and laughing sometimes in delight, Charu entered the room.

The thread of the story was broken. That her arrival had interrupted a lively conversation Charu saw quite plainly.

Amal asked, 'Bouthan, you returned so early?'

Charu said, 'So I see. I've returned too early.' She turned to leave.

Amal said, 'You did a good thing, you saved me. I was thinking, who knows when you'll be back. I have brought Manmatha Dutta's new book, *Evening Bird*, to read to you.'

Charu: Let it be for now. I've got work to do.

Amal: If you have work, order me, I'll do it.

Charu knew Amal would buy the book today and come to read it to her; Charu, in order to make Amal envious, would praise Manmatha's writing and Amal would read the book in an unnatural pronunciation and ridicule it. Imagining all this and becoming impatient, she had transgressed all the rules of courtesy at the house where she had been invited, and offering illness as an excuse, had returned home. Now she repeatedly thinks, 'I was fine there. It was wrong of me to come away.'

Manda was also so shameless. Sitting alone in the room with Amal and laughing. What would people say if they saw this? But to scold Manda about this was difficult for Charu. The reason was, what if Manda gave Charu's example in reply. But Charu herself was one thing, Manda another. Charu encourages Amal in his writing, discusses literature with him, but those are not Manda's intentions. Manda is doubtless spreading a net to enchant this simple young boy. To save Amal from this great danger was Charu's responsibility. How will she explain this deceptive woman's intentions to Amal? If she does explain, what if he does not stop being enticed and the very opposite happens?

Poor Dada! He is killing himself working on her husband's paper night and day, and Manda is sitting in a corner trying to entice Amal. Dada is quite untroubled. He has immense faith in Manda. How could Charu see all this with her own eyes and be silent. It was completely wrong.

But Amal was fine before, from the day he started writing, from that day all the trouble had begun. Charu herself was the source of his writing. What an inauspicious moment that was when she had encouraged it. Now could she have the same influence on him as before? Now Amal had tasted the pleasure of being appreciated by many, it would make no difference to him if there was one person less among them.

Charu understood clearly that the imminent danger for Amal was falling from her hands into the hands of many. Charu is no longer an equal for Amal; he has left Charu behind. This has to be redressed.

Oh, simple Amal, deceptive Manda, poor Dada.

6

THAT DAY THE NEW CLOUDS OF ASHAR HAD COVERED THE sky. The darkness inside the room had deepened so Charu was sitting near the open window, bent over, writing something.

She did not know when it was that Amal came in without a sound and stood behind her. In the gentle light of the rain Charu went on writing, Amal went on reading. Nearby there were one or two of Amal's published compositions lying open; to Charu, those were the only ideals for her own writing.

'Why do you say you can't write!'

Suddenly hearing Amal's voice Charu was very startled; quickly she hid the notebook; she said, 'That was very wrong of you.'

Amal: How is it wrong of me?

Charu: Why did you hide behind me and read it?

Amal: Because I don't get the chance to read it openly.

Charu was about to tear up her writing. Amal quickly snatched the notebook from her hands. Charu said, 'If you read it I'll never speak to you again.'

Amal: If you don't let me read it I'll never speak to you again.

Charu: Please don't read it, Thakurpo.

In the end it was Charu who had to admit defeat. She had been restless to show her work to Amal, but she had not thought she would feel so embarrassed at the time of showing it to him. When Amal, after many entreaties, began to read, Charu's hands and feet became cold with embarrassment. She said, 'I'll bring some paan.' She quickly went to the next room as if to make paan.

Amal finished reading and went to Charu and said, 'It's marvellous.'

Charu, forgetting to put the bits of supari nut in the paan, said, 'There's no need to joke. Give me my notebook.'

Amal said, 'I won't give you the notebook now, I'll copy the work and send it to a magazine!'

Charu: What! Send it to a magazine! You can't do that.

Charu made a lot of noise. Amal also would not let up. When he repeatedly swore that 'It was good enough to send to a magazine', then Charu, as if extremely dejected, said, 'It's impossible to win with you. Whatever you take on you refuse to let go of.'

Amal said, 'I have to show this to Dada.'

Hearing this Charu stopped making paan and quickly stood up; trying to snatch the notebook away, she said, 'No, you can't read it to him. If you tell him about my writing then I won't write one word more.'

Amal: Bouthan, you misunderstand. Whatever Dada may say, when he sees your writing he will be very happy.

Charu: That may be, but I don't have any use for that happiness.

Charu had vowed that she would write; she would amaze Amal; she would not rest without proving how different she was from Manda. These few days she has written plenty and torn it up. Whatever she writes becomes very much like Amal's work; when she compares she sees certain parts have been completely lifted from Amal's compositions. These parts are good, the remaining are amateurish. If Amal saw it he would laugh inside. Imagining this Charu tore up all that writing into little bits and threw it into the pond, for fear that even a remnant of it should come into Amal's hands.

At first she had written, 'Shravan's Clouds.' She had thought, 'I have created a truly new piece, drenched in emotion and tears.' Suddenly, coming back to herself, she saw that the composition was almost exactly like Amal's 'Ashar's Moon.' Amal has written, 'Oh moon, why are you hiding among the clouds like a thief?' Charu had written, 'Oh clouds, from where have you so suddenly come to hide the moon beneath your blue anchal and run away,' etc.

Unable to get out of the arena of Amal's writing Charu changed the subject of her compositions. Moon, clouds, the shefali flower, the bau-katha-kao bird, abandoning all this she wrote a piece called 'Kalitala.' In Charu's village, near the pond dark with shadows, there was a Kali temple; all her childhood imaginings surrounding that temple; her fears, excitements, her specific memories about it, the old, eternal tales in the village about the greatness of that deity—she wrote a piece about all of this. The beginning was full of pompous poetry in Amal's style, but as soon as she moved further, her writing easily became simple and filled with the language, manners and texture of a village.

This was the composition Amal snatched away and read. He thought the beginning was well written, but the poetry had not been sustained till the end. Whatever it may be, for a first piece the authoress's effort was commendable.

Charu said, 'Thakurpo, come let's start a monthly magazine. What do you say?'

Amal: How can the magazine run without a lot of money?

Charu: This magazine of ours won't cost anything. It won't be printed you see—we will write it by hand. No one else's work will be published in it except yours and mine, it won't be given to anyone else to read. Only two copies will be made, one for you, one for me.

Had it been a while ago, Amal would have been excited by this proposal; now the excitement of secrecy has left him. Now, unless he aims his work at many readers he gets no pleasure. Still, in order to preserve an old custom, he expressed his enthusiasm. He said, 'It'll be fun.'

Charu said, 'But you have to promise that you won't publish your work anywhere but in our magazine.'

Amal: Then the editors of other journals will kill me.

Charu: And don't I have weapons with which to kill?

So the discussion went. Two editors, two writers and two readers got together to form a committee.

Amal said, 'The name of the magazine will be "Charupath".'

Charu said, 'No, its name will be "Amala".'

This new arrangement made Charu forget the sorrow and annoyance of the last few days. In their monthly journal there was no way for Manda to enter; and its door was closed even to the outside world.

7

ONE DAY BHUPATI CAME TO CHARU AND SAID, 'CHARU, THAT you would become an authoress, this we had not agreed on before!'

Charu, startled and blushing, said, 'Me, an authoress! Who told you! Never!'

Bhupati: Caught with stolen goods. The proof is right here.

He took out a volume of *Sarorohu*. Charu saw, all the writing she had thought to be their secret property and was collecting in their handwritten monthly magazine, had now been published in *Sarorohu*, with the names of the author and the authoress.

Charu felt as if someone had opened the door of a cage and made her dear tamed birds fly away. Forgetting the embarrassment of being caught by Bhupati, she began to feel extremely angry at the traitorous Amal.

'And look at this.' Bhupati opened the newspaper *Vishwabandhu,* and held it in front of Charu. In it there was an essay on 'The Style of Contemporary Bengali Writing.'

Charu pushed away the paper with her hand and said, 'Why should I read this?' At this time, she was so upset with Amal that she could not pay attention to anything else. Bhupati insisted and said, 'Read it once and see.'

Charu was forced to glance through the article. The author has written a harsh piece criticising the pompous prose of certain contemporary writers. In it the critic has expressed great contempt for the style of Amal and Manmatha Dutta. He has compared their style with the simple, natural style of the new authoress, Srimati Charubala, whose spontaneous feeling and descriptive skill he has praised profusely. He has written, the salvation of Amal and company lies in following this mode of writing and succeeding, otherwise there is no doubt that they are bound to fail completely.

Bhupati laughed and said, 'This is called learning that overtakes the teacher.'

Charu, at this first praise for her writing, was on the point of feeling a certain joy. But repeatedly the joy came and turned to pain. Her mind and heart refused to be made happy in any way. As soon as the cup filled with the draught of praise came near, she pushed it away.

She understood that Amal had wanted to surprise her by publishing her work in the magazine. In the end, after it was published, he had decided that when a paper printed an article praising the work, he would show her both together and calm her anger as well as fuel her enthusiasm. When the favourable review came, why didn't Amal come eagerly to show it to her? This criticism has hurt Amal and because he does not want to show it to Charu he has kept these papers absolutely secret. The tiny literary nest that she had quietly created for her own joy was suddenly hit by a large piece of hail from the hailstorm of this praise and destroyed. Charu did not like this at all.

After Bhupati left, Charu sat quietly on her bed for a long time; *Sarorohu* and *Vishwabandhu* lay open before her.

Notebook in hand, Amal came from behind, soundlessly, in order to startle Charu. He came near and saw Charu absorbed in thought with the *Vishwabandhu* article in front of her.

Amal went away, again soundlessly. 'They have criticised me and praised Charu so she is senseless with joy.' In moments his whole being seemed to turn bitter. There was no doubt that Charu, reading the criticism of an idiot, was thinking herself to be greater than her teacher. Being sure of this, Amal became very angry with Charu. Charu should have torn up all those papers to shreds and burnt them to ashes in the fire. Angry with Charu, Amal came and stood in front of Manda's room and called loudly, 'Manda Bouthan.'

Manda: Come, come. Today I get to see you without asking for you. What good fortune I have today.

Amal: Would you like to hear one or two of my new compositions?

Manda: For so many days you have been promising to read it, but you haven't. There's no need—one doesn't know who might get angry and then you'll be in trouble—it's no problem for me.

Amal said, somewhat sharply, 'Who will get angry? Why will they get angry? We'll see about that. Come and listen now.'

Manda sat down as if with great eagerness. Amal began to read in a somewhat grandiose manner.

Amal's writing was extremely foreign to Manda, she was completely at sea with it. For this reason she brought a joyous smile to her face and began to listen eagerly. Amal's voice became even louder in its enthusiasm.

He was reading, 'Abhimanyu, when he was in the womb, learnt how to enter a line of battle, but not how to emerge from it—in the same way the river's flow, when it was in the stone womb of the mountain, learnt only to go forward, but not to turn back. Alas, river's flow, alas youth, alas time, alas world, you can only go forward—the road on which you scatter the gold and jewels of your memories, that road you never look back on. Only the human heart looks back, the eternal world never turns to look that way.'

At this time a shadow fell near Manda's door. That shadow Manda saw. But, pretending as if she hadn't seen it, she continued looking at Amal steadily, listening to him with a profound attention.

The shadow immediately moved away.

Charu was waiting; as soon as Amal came she would properly castigate *Vishwabandhu* as it deserved to be and scold Amal for breaking his vow and publishing their work in a monthly journal.

The time for Amal's coming passed, yet there was no sign of him. Charu had kept a composition ready; she wanted to read it to Amal; it too lay there.

At this time, from somewhere, came the sound of Amal's voice. It seemed like Manda's room. She got up as if struck by an arrow. Soundlessly she came and stood near the door of Manda's room. The piece Amal was reading to Manda Charu had not heard yet. Amal was reading—'Only the human heart looks behind, the eternal world never turns to look that way.'

Charu could not go away as soundlessly as she had come. Today, one blow after another took away her patience. That Manda did not understand a word and Amal, like an ignorant idiot, was reading to her and getting satisfaction from it, this fact she felt like shouting out loud. But without saying it, she expressed it through her angry footsteps. Going into her bedroom she slammed the door shut.

Amal stopped reading for a few moments. Manda laughed and indicated in Charu's direction. Amal said to himself, 'What tyranny is this on Bouthan's part? Has she decided I'm her slave? I can't read to anyone but her. This is a tremendous oppression.' Thinking this he began to read to Manda even more loudly.

When he finished reading, he passed by Charu's room and went away. He looked once and saw the door was closed.

Charu heard the footsteps and knew Amal was passing by her room. He didn't stop even once. Anger and pain kept back her tears. Taking out the notebook full of her new writing she tore to shreds every page and made a heap of the pieces. What an inauspicious moment it was when all this writing began.

8

At twilight the fragrance of jasmine arises from the flower pots on the balcony. Through the torn clouds there could be seen stars in a fresh, tender sky. Today, Charu has not tied her hair, has not changed her clothes. She sits at the window in the darkness, a gentle wind slowly blows her loose hair, and from her eyes why tears are flowing in this way she herself is unable to understand.

At this time, Bhupati entered the room. His face was extremely pale, his heart heavy. This was not the time when Bhupati usually returned. After writing for the paper and checking proofs, it was often late by the time he came to the inner rooms. Today, immediately after twilight, in the hope of who knows what consolation, he had come to Charu.

In the room the lamp was not lit. In the little light from the open window Bhupati dimly saw Charu; he slowly came and stood behind her. Even when she heard footsteps Charu did not turn her head—she continued sitting like a statue, still and stiff.

Bhupati, somewhat surprised, said, 'Charu.'

Startled by Bhupati's voice, she sat up. She had not realised it was Bhupati. Bhupati ran his fingers through her hair and in a voice soft with affection, asked, 'In the darkness you're sitting alone. Where's Manda?'

Whatever Charu had hoped for, none of it happened during the course of the whole day. She was sure that Amal would come and ask her forgiveness—for that she had prepared herself and was waiting; at this time, hearing the unexpected sound of Bhupati's voice, she could not control herself any longer—she began to cry.

Bhupati, anxious, pained, asked, 'Charu, what has happened, Charu?'

What has happened that is difficult to say. What is it that has happened? Amal did not show his writing first to her but to Manda, how could she complain about this to Bhupati? Wouldn't Bhupati laugh when he heard it? In this insignificant incident, the reason for serious complaint was hiding in a place that was impossible for Charu to find. Without reason, why she was feeling so much pain, this very fact she could not completely understand and so the sharpness of her pain increased even more.

Bhupati: Tell me, Charu, what has happened to you? Have I wronged you in any way? You know how busy I am with the paper and its problems, if I have hurt you in any way I haven't done it intentionally.

Bhupati was asking questions about something to which there were no replies to be given, because of this Charu became impatient inside, if Bhupati would free her from this and leave she would be relieved.

Bhupati, not receiving a reply for the second time, again said in a voice full of affection, 'I can't always come to you, Charu. For that I am guilty, but it will not happen any more. From now on I will not be with the paper night and day. You will get as much of me as you want.'

Charu, impatient, said, 'Not because of that.'

Bhupati said, 'Then because of what?' and sat down on the bed.

Charu, unable to hide her annoyance, said, 'Let it be now. I'll tell you at night.'

Bhupati for a moment became very still, then said, 'Alright, let it be for now.' Saying this he got up slowly and went out. He had come here with something of his own to say, but it did not get said.

That Bhupati was hurt, Charu knew. She thought, 'I'll call him back.' But what will she call him back and say? Repentance pierced her, but she found no solution.

Night came. Today Charu, with special care, arranged Bhupati's dinner and, fan in hand, sat waiting.

At this time she heard Manda shouting loudly, 'Braja, Braja.' When Braja, the servant, replied, she asked, 'Has Amalbabu finished eating?' Braja replied, 'Yes, he has.' Manda said, 'He has finished eating yet you haven't taken him his paan.' Manda began to reproach Braja.

At this time Bhupati came to the inner rooms and sat down to eat his dinner. Charu began to fan him.

Charu had vowed today that she would speak happily and affectionately to Bhupati. She had already thought of the things she would say. But the sound of Manda's voice destroyed all her detailed arrangements, and at mealtime she could not say a word to Bhupati. Bhupati was also very melancholy and absentminded. He did not eat properly, Charu only asked once, 'Why aren't you eating anything.'

Bhupati protested and said, 'Why? I haven't eaten very little.'

In the bedroom when they were together, Bhupati said, 'You said you'd tell me something tonight.'

Charu said, 'Look, for sometime I haven't been liking Manda's behaviour. I feel uneasy about keeping her here any longer.'

Bhupati: Why? What has she done?

Charu: The way she is with Amal, it's embarrassing to see.

Bhupati laughed and said, 'You're mad. Amal is so young—'

Charu: You don't keep up with any news at home, you only gather news from outside. Whatever it may be, I am concerned about Dada. When he eats or doesn't eat Manda doesn't even care to know, but if the arrangements for Amal are not perfect she scolds the servants and troubles them.

Bhupati: I must say, you women really are very suspicious.

Angered, Charu said, 'Alright we are suspicious, but I'm telling you I will not allow this brazen shamelessness in the house.'

Bhupati laughed secretly at all these baseless suspicions of Charu's and was also pleased. So that the home remained pure, so that the ordered arena of conjugality was not tarnished, even touched in the least by any probable or imaginary stain—for this the extreme alertness of virtuous wives, and their fervently suspicious glances, all had a sweet and noble quality about them.

Bhupati, filled with respect and affection, kissed Charu's forehead and said, 'There is no need to worry about this. Umapati is going away to Mymensingh to set up his practice, he is taking Manda with him.'

In the end, to get rid of his own worries and all this unpleasant talk, Bhupati took a notebook from the table and said, 'Read me your writing, Charu.'

Charu snatched the notebook from him and said, 'You won't like this. You'll joke about it.'

Bhupati was somewhat hurt by these words, but hiding it he smiled and said, 'Alright, I won't joke, I'll listen so silently you'll have the illusion I've fallen asleep.'

But Bhupati was not indulged—soon the notebook disappeared beneath coverings and clothes.

9

Bhupati had not been able to tell Charu everything. Umapati was the supervisor for Bhupati's newspaper. Getting donations, paying back debts to the printers and to creditors in the market, giving the servants their salaries, all of this was Umapati's responsibility.

Meanwhile, Bhupati was amazed to suddenly receive a lawyer's letter from the paper dealer. They had let him know that he owed them Rs 2,700. Bhupati called Umapati and said, 'What is this? I've already given you this money. We should not be owing more than four or five hundred rupees for paper.'

Umapati said, 'They must have made a mistake.'

But things could not be suppressed any longer. For a while Umapati has been deceiving Bhupati in this way. Not only regarding the paper; in Bhupati's name he has amassed many debts in the market. In the village he is building a house of concrete, some of the material for that he has bought in

Bhupati's name, most of it he has paid for from the money for the paper.

When he was found guilty beyond a doubt he said, in a harsh voice, 'I am not disappearing. I'll work and repay you slowly—even if an anna of debt remains to you then my name is not Umapati.'

Bhupati was not consoled by the inviolability of Umapati's name. It was not the loss of money that saddened Bhupati so much, but at this unexpected betrayal he seemed to step out of a house and into a void.

In the morning he had gone to the inner rooms. There was one place in the world in which he could completely trust; his heart had become impatient to go and experience that place for a moment. At the time, Charu, full of her own sorrow, had extinguished the evening lamp and was sitting near the window.

The very next day Umapati was ready to leave for Mymensingh. Before the creditors in the market came to know anything, he wanted to slip away. Bhupati, filled with aversion, did not talk to Umapati—that silence of Bhupati's Umapati regarded as fortunate.

Amal came and asked, 'Manda Bouthan, what is this? Why are you packing all your things?'

Manda: Oh, we have to go. We won't stay forever, will we?

Amal: Where are you going?

Manda: Home.

Amal: Why? What was the problem here?

Manda: Why should I have problems? I was with all of you, I was happy. But someone else had problems.

She said this and looked insinuatingly at Charu's room.

Amal became grave and quiet. Manda said, 'How embarrassing! What will Babu think!'

Amal did not say any more. This much he understood, Charu had said something about them to Dada that should not have been said.

Amal left the house and began to walk the streets. He desired not to return to this house again. If Dada had believed Bouthan and found him guilty, then he would have to take the same road as Manda. To bid farewell to Manda was in a way an order for his own banishment—it was only that it hadn't been actually said. After this his path of action was absolutely clear—he could not stay here a moment longer. But that Dada would harbour in his mind a completely wrong notion about him, he could not bear. For so long, with unbroken trust, he has given Amal a place in his house and supported him. How could he leave without explaining to Dada that he had not breached this trust in any way?

At that time Bhupati, his forehead in his palm, was deep in thought about the ungratefulness of relatives, the urging of his creditors, unmanageable accounts and an empty coffer. In this harsh grief he had no companion—he was readying himself to stand up alone and fight the pain and the debts.

At this time Amal, like a storm, entered the room. Bhupati, startled out of his own bottomless worries, looked at Amal.

He said, 'What news, Amal?' Suddenly he thought, maybe Amal has brought some more bad news.

Amal said, 'Dada, do you have any reason to doubt me?'

Bhupati said, surprised, 'Doubt you?' In his mind he thought, 'The way the world is showing itself I may even be doubting Amal some day, it won't be surprising.'

Amal: Has Bouthan complained to you in any way about my character?

Bhupati thought, Oh it is this. I am saved. It's the hurtful pride of love. He had thought that over and above this disaster there would be another one, but even in times of great hardship these small matters must be paid attention to.

If it were at another time, Bhupati would have ridiculed Amal, but today he did not have that cheerfulness, he said, 'Are you crazy?'

Amal again asked, 'Bouthan hasn't said anything?'

Bhupati: If she has said something because she loves you there is no reason to get angry about it.

Amal: I should go elsewhere now and start looking for some work.

Bhupati scolded him, saying, 'Amal, don't be so juvenile. You should study now, work will come later.'

Amal, with a darkened face, came out. Bhupati began to examine tables of subscribers' accounts over the last three years.

10

AMAL DECIDED THAT HE WOULD HAVE TO SETTLE THINGS with Bouthan, and until this thing came to an end, he would not let it go. The harsh words he would have to say to Bouthan he began to recite to himself in his mind.

After Manda's departure Charu decided she would herself send for Amal and pacify his anger. But she would have to use a piece of writing as the excuse. Imitating a work of Amal's, she began an essay called, 'Light of the Moonless Night'. Charu understood that Amal did not like any original, innovative writing of hers.

The full moon reveals all her light and Charu in her new essay reproaches the moon for this. She writes—In the unfathomable darkness of the moonless night the sixteen phases of the moon are contained in all its stages, not even a ray is lost. So, more than the full moon, it is the darkness of the moonless night which is more complete, etc.

Amal reveals all his writings to everyone, Charu does not do that—in the comparison between a full moon night and a moonless night, is there a reference to that?

Meanwhile, a third person in the household, Bhupati, to free himself from an impending debt, went to his close friend Motilal.

In a time of difficulty for Motilal, Bhupati had lent him a few thousand rupees—that day, very troubled, he went to ask for the money back. Motilal, after his bath, was sitting bare-bodied and enjoying the breeze from a fan. On a small wooden box he had spread out a sheet of paper and was writing, in very small letters, the name of Durga. Seeing Bhupati he said in a tone of great cordiality, 'Come, come—one hardly sees you these days.'

Hearing about the money Motilal thought long and hard and said, 'What money are you talking about? Have I taken anything from you recently?'

When Bhupati reminded him of the year and the date Motilal said, 'Oh, that has been settled a long time ago.'

In Bhupati's eyes the appearance of everything around him seemed to change. Bhupati looked at that part of the world from which a mask had fallen away, and fear made his body tense. When a flood comes suddenly, a man runs in fear towards whatever is the highest point around; Bhupati fled from the uncertain external world and entered the inner rooms in the same way; he said to himself, 'Whatever else happens, Charu will never deceive you.'

Charu, at that time, was sitting on the bed with a pillow on her lap and a notebook on the pillow. She was bent over the notebook, writing. When Bhupati came and stood very close to her she seemed to come back to herself, she quickly put the notebook under her legs.

When there is sorrow inside then the smallest blow brings great pain. Seeing the unnecessary swiftness with which Charu hid her writing, Bhupati felt hurt.

Bhupati slowly sat on the bed next to Charu. Charu, at this unexpected obstacle to her writing, and in the anxiety of hiding her notebook, became embarrassed and could think of nothing to say.

That day, Bhupati had nothing of his own to give or say. He had come empty handed to Charu, as one does in prayer. If from Charu he had received even one question born of love and concern, any affection, the pain of his wounds would have received a balm. But at a moment's notice Charu could not find anywhere the key to the storehouse of her love. The strained speechlessness of both made the silence in the room extremely dense.

After a time of complete silence, Bhupati, taking a deep breath, got up, left the bed and very slowly walked out.

At that time Amal, with various difficult words loaded in his mind, was coming quickly towards Charu's room. On the way he saw Bhupati's withered, pale face and, stopping anxiously, asked, 'Dada, are you ill?'

Hearing Amal's soft voice suddenly Bhupati's whole heart, with all its tears, seemed to swell inside him. For a while, no words emerged. With great strength, controlling himself,

Bhupati said in a voice filled with sorrow, 'Nothing's wrong, Amal. Is there any new work of yours about to be published?'

The difficult words that Amal had gathered, where did they go? Quickly he came to Charu's room and asked, 'Bouthan, tell me what's happened to Dada?'

Charu said, 'Why, I didn't notice anything. Another paper must have criticised his.' Amal shook his head.

Without sending for him Amal had come and had easily started a conversation. Seeing this Charu was relieved and happy. Immediately she started talking about writing—she said, 'Today I've written a piece called "Light of the Moonless Night"; he almost saw it.'

Charu had decided that Amal would beg to see her new composition. In that expectation, she even played with the notebook a little. But Amal looked once, sharply, at Charu's face—what he understood, what he thought, is unknown. He got up, startled. Walking on mountain roads suddenly the mist cleared and the traveller, surprised, saw—he was about to step into an abyss a hundred hands deep. Amal, without saying anything, left the room.

Charu did not understand the significance of this unprecedented behaviour.

11

THE DAY AFTER, AT AN UNEXPECTED HOUR, BHUPATI AGAIN came to the bedroom and sent for Charu. He said, 'There is a good marriage proposal for Amal.'

Charu was absentminded. She said, 'Good what?'

Bhupati: Marriage proposal.

Charu: Why, wasn't I good enough?

Bhupati laughed loudly. He said, 'Whether you are good enough or not Amal hasn't yet been asked. Even if he did like you I do have some small rights, I'm not letting them go so easily.

Charu: Oh, what are you talking about? You just said you received a marriage proposal. Charu blushed.

Bhupati: If that were so, would I run to you with the news? I wouldn't have expected a reward for that.

Charu: Amal has received a marriage proposal. Fine, good. Then, why delay?

Bhupati: The lawyer, Raghunathbabu, from Bardhaman, wishes to marry his daughter to Amal and send him to England.

Charu, amazed, asked, 'England?'

Bhupati: Yes, England.

Charu: Amal will go to England. What fun. Good, very good. So tell him about it.

Bhupati: Before I do, why don't you call him and tell him once.

Charu: I've told him three thousand times. He doesn't listen to me. I can't tell him.

Bhupati: What do you think? He won't agree?

Charu: We've tried many times before, there was no way he would agree.

Bhupati: But he should not let go of this proposal. I have a lot of debts now, I cannot give shelter to Amal as I used to.

Bhupati sent for Amal. When Amal came he said, 'The lawyer, Raghunathbabu, from Bardhaman, has sent a proposal of marriage for you, he would like you to marry his daughter. He wants to send you to England after the wedding. What do you think?'

Amal said, 'If you approve, I will not disagree.' Hearing Amal's words, both of them were surprised.

No one had expected him to agree at once.

In a sharp voice, Charu began to ridicule Amal and said,'If Dada consents then he will agree. What an obedient younger brother. Where was your devotion to Dada all these days, Thakurpo?'

Amal did not reply, he tried to smile a little.

To rouse Amal from his state of non-reply Charu said, even more sharply, 'Instead, why don't you say you desire it yourself. Why did you have to pretend all these days that you didn't want to get married? Hunger in the stomach, shyness at the lips.'

Bhupati said jokingly, 'It was for your sake that he was suppressing his hunger, in case you became jealous hearing about a sister-in-law.'

At this Charu blushed and said angrily, 'Jealousy! Really! I never feel jealous. You shouldn't say things like that.'

Bhupati: Look at that, I can't even joke with my own wife.

Charu: No. I don't like that kind of joking.

Bhupati: Alright. I've made a grave mistake. Forgive me. Anyway, the marriage is then decided on?

Amal said, 'Yes.'

Charu: You couldn't even wait to find out whether the girl is good or bad. You didn't even faintly express that you had reached such a state.

Bhupati: Amal, if you want to see the girl I can arrange it. I've been told the girl is beautiful.

Amal: No, I don't want to see her.

Charu: Why do you listen to him? Can there be a marriage without seeing the bride first? If he doesn't want to see her, we will.

Amal: No, Dada. There is no need to create a false delay with this.

Charu: No need—a delay will break his heart. Why don't you put on your topar and leave right now. Who knows, someone might snatch away your precious jewel.

None of Charu's jokes had any effect on Amal.

Charu: Is it that you can't wait to go away to England? Why, were we beating and flogging you here? Unless they can put on a hat and coat and become a sahib, today's young boys don't feel satisfied. Thakurpo, when you come back from England will you recognise us dark-skinned people?

Amal: What would be the point of going to England then?

Bhupati: It is to forget the dark-skinned self that seven seas must be crossed. But why be afraid, we will still be here, there will be no scarcity of the dark-skinned people's devotees.

Bhupati, very happy, immediately wrote back to Bardhaman. The wedding date was decided.

12

Meanwhile, the paper had to be closed down. Bhupati could not bear its expenses any more. Named 'The Common Man', this huge, merciless thing to which he had endlessly, day and night, single-mindedly devoted himself, had to be abandoned in a single minute. All the endeavour of Bhupati's life for the last twelve years, the habitual road it has been following without a break, that road, at a certain point, found itself surrounded by water. For this Bhupati was not at all prepared. Suddenly stalled, where could he take back all his efforts of so many days? Like starving orphan children they seemed to be staring at Bhupati's face, Bhupati brought them to his own inner rooms and stood them before a kind, caring woman.

The woman was thinking about something. She was saying to herself, 'How surprising this is. Amal is getting married, that is very good. But after so long he will leave us and go to someone else's house to marry, did not this bring about, even once, a little hesitation in his mind? For so long we have taken such care of him, and the moment he gets a chance to leave, he instantly readies himself, as if all this time he was waiting for an opportunity. Yet how pleasant are his words, so filled with love. It is hard to know a person. Who would have thought that the person who is able to write so well has nothing in his heart.'

Comparing her own heart's abundance to Amal's, Charu tried to scorn Amal's emptiness of heart but she couldn't do it. Inside, a constant pain like a burning spear began to continuously increase her hurtful pride—Amal will leave in a few days yet he is nowhere to be seen. There is no time to resolve the disagreement that has come between us. Every moment Charu thinks that Amal will come on his own—the pleasant times they have known for so long will not end in this way, but Amal still does not come. In the end, when the day for Amal's leaving drew near, Charu herself sent for Amal.

Amal sent a reply, 'I will come after a little while.' Charu went and sat on a stool on the balcony where they always sat. From the morning it has been cloudy and sultry—Charu takes her hair and knots it loosely at the neck, takes a hand fan and gently fans her tired body.

It was very late. Eventually her hand fan moved no more. Anger, grief and impatience rose in her heart. In her mind she said—Let Amal not come, so what. Yet, at the sound of footsteps her attention immediately went towards the door.

In the far church the bells rang eleven o'clock. After his bath, Bhupati would now come for lunch. There is still half an hour left, even if now Amal would come. No matter how, their silent quarrel would have to be settled today—she could not say farewell to Amal in this way. The long, sweet relationship between this brother-in-law and sister-in-law—so much affection, childish quarrelling, the tyranny born of this affection, an awning made from the leaves and creepers of so much intimate, tranquil and happy conversation, throwing an everlasting protective shade over everything—will Amal crush this in the dust and go away for so long, so far? Will he not regret it even a little? Will he not sprinkle even a last bit of water near its roots—water from the final tears of their long relationship?

Half an hour has almost passed. Opening up the loose knot of her hair, Charu took some of it and began rapidly winding it around her fingers. The tears can no longer be held back. The servant came and said, 'You have to take out a coconut for Babu.'

Charu threw down the keys to the pantry which were tied to her anchal—the servant, surprised, went away with them.

From near Charu's heart, something was rising to her throat.

At this time, a smiling Bhupati came to have his lunch. Charu, fan in hand, came to where he was eating and saw Amal with him. Charu did not look at him.

Amal asked, 'Bouthan, did you send for me?'

Charu said, 'No, there's no need anymore.'

Amal: Then I will leave. I have a lot to arrange.

Charu then looked with shining eyes at Amal's face; she said, 'Alright.'

Amal looked once at Charu's face and left.

After lunch Bhupati usually spends some time with Charu. Today he is very busy with his accounts so he cannot stay long in the inner rooms. Somewhat regretfully, he said, 'I cannot stay for long today—today there are a lot of problems.'

Charu said, 'So, go then.'

Bhupati thought, Charu is hurt. He said, 'That doesn't mean I have to go right now, I have to rest a little.' Saying this he sat down. He saw that Charu was depressed. He sat for a long time, repentantly, but he could not get a conversation going. After a long time of trying to begin a conversation he said, 'Amal is leaving tomorrow, for a while you will feel very alone.'

Charu did not reply to this and, as if to bring something, went into another room. Bhupati waited for a few minutes and went out.

Charu today looked at Amal's face and noticed he had become very thin over these few days—on his face there was no longer that bloom of youth. This brought Charu happiness and grief. That the coming separation was bringing Amal pain, Charu did not doubt—yet why was Amal behaving like this? Why was he staying away from her? Why was he deliberately making this farewell time so full of bitter confrontation?

Lying in bed and thinking she was suddenly startled. Suddenly she remembered Manda. Perhaps it was like this, Amal loved Manda. It was because Manda had left that Amal was like this. No! Amal's mind could not be like that. So small? So soiled? He would be attracted towards a married woman? She tried single-mindedly to banish the suspicion but the suspicion remained with a biting strength.

In this way the time for farewell came. The clouds did not clear. Amal came and said in a shaking voice, 'Bouthan, it is time for me to leave. From now on look after Dada. He is going through a difficult time—besides you he has no other road to solace.

Amal, seeing Bhupati's melancholy, darkened face, had enquired and found out about his misfortunes. How Bhupati was alone battling with sorrow and adversity, how he had not received solace or help from anyone, yet did not let the relatives he sheltered be affected by this disaster, Amal thought of all this and kept silent. Then he thought of Charu, he thought of himself, his ears reddened, he said, with emotion, 'To hell with "Ashar's Moon" and "Light of the Moonless Night". If I can become a barrister and help Dada, only then am I a man.'

Last night Charu had stayed up the entire night thinking of what she would say to Amal at leaving time—with a smiling hurtful pride and happy indifference she had polished those words in her mind till they were sharp and shining. But at the time of saying farewell no words emerged from Charu. She only said, 'You will write, won't you, Amal?'

Amal put his head on the ground and touched her feet. Charu ran into her bedroom and closed the door.

13

Bhupati went to Bardhaman and, after Amal's wedding, saw him off to England and returned home.

Blows from all sides had made the trusting Bhupati detached from the outside world. Meetings, gatherings, socialising, he no longer enjoyed any of it. He thought, 'With all this I have only fooled myself. For so long life's joyous days passed by in vain and their best part I threw away.'

Bhupati said to himself, 'The paper is gone. Good. I am free.' The way birds return to their nests at twilight, when the evening is about to begin, in the same way Bhupati abandoned his lifelong arena of action and came to the inner rooms where Charu was. In his mind he decided, 'Enough. Now, no going anywhere else, my existence is here. The paper ship I have always played with has sunk, now I will go home.'

Bhupati had a belief held by many; no one had to earn a right over his wife, a wife, like the North Star, keeps her own light always lit—the wind does not blow it out, it does not wait for fuel. When the outside began to crumble, Bhupati did not even think of examining the arches and vaults of the inner rooms to see whether there too the cracks had begun.

Bhupati returned home from Bardhaman in the evening. He washed his hands and face and hurriedly ate an early dinner. Charu would naturally be eager to hear every last detail about Amal's wedding and his leaving for England, so Bhupati made no delay. He went to the bedroom and began to pull at the infinitely long pipe of his hookah. Charu was still absent. Perhaps she was busy with housework. He was tired and the smoking made him sleepy. Every few minutes he would wake, startled, from his drowsiness and wonder, 'Why hasn't Charu come yet?' In the end, Bhupati, unable to wait, called for Charu. He asked her, 'Charu, why are you so late today?'

Charu gave no explanation. She said, 'Yes, I'm late today.'

Bhupati waited for Charu's eager questions. Charu did not ask any. At this, Bhupati was upset. Does this mean Charu does not love Amal? Till Amal was here Charu would delight in being with him, and as soon as he went away she became so indifferent! This contradictory behaviour gave rise to certain misgivings in his mind, he began to think—does this mean Charu has no depth of heart? Does she only know how to enjoy herself, is she not capable of love? Such detachment in a woman is not a good thing.

Bhupati was happy at Charu and Amal's friendship. Their childlike quarrels and making up, playing and plotting, seemed sweet and wonderful to him. Charu always took care of Amal, she indulged him, and Bhupati saw this as Charu's gentle kindness and was happy. Today he was surprised and thought, was all that superficial, did it have no foundations in the heart? If Charu was heartless, thought Bhupati, where would he take shelter?

Little by little, to examine her, Bhupati made conversation. 'Charu, have you been well? You aren't ill, are you?'

Charu's reply was brief. 'I am well.'

Bhupati: So Amal's wedding is done.

Saying this Bhupati became silent; Charu tried hard to say something appropriate, but no words emerged; she remained stiffly quiet.

Bhupati, because of his very nature, did not notice anything sharply—but because the sorrow of Amal's departure was affecting him, Charu's indifference hurt. He wanted to talk about Amal to a Charu who was equally pained by his departure and so lighten the heaviness of his own heart.

Bhupati: The girl is rather pleasant looking. Charu, are you asleep?

Charu said, 'No.'

Bhupati: Poor Amal, went away all alone. When I put him on board he began to cry like a child. Seeing that, me in my old age, I couldn't hold back my tears. There were two Englishmen on board, they were so amused to see grown men cry.

With the lamps extinguished, in the darkness of the bedroom, Charu turned around and rested on her side, then hurriedly left the bed. Bhupati, startled, asked, 'Charu, are you ill?'

Receiving no answer, Bhupati also left the bed. From the veranda nearby there came the sound of muffled crying. Bhupati rushed to the veranda and saw Charu sprawled on the ground, trying to stop her tears.

This extreme outburst of grief amazed Bhupati. He thought, how much I had misunderstood Charu. Charu's nature is so reserved that even to me she does not want to reveal her heart's pain. Those whose nature is like this are capable of very deep love and their pain is also very great. Charu's love, unlike that of ordinary women, is not completely visible from the outside, Bhupati recognised this. Bhupati had never seen the upsurge of Charu's love; today he understood, very specifically, the reason was that the expanse of Charu's love was deep inside her. Bhupati himself was inept at the outer expression of his emotions; becoming acquainted with the deep, hidden quality of Charu's passion, he felt very pleased.

Bhupati then sat next to Charu and without saying a word began to gently caress her. How to console someone, Bhupati did not know. He did not understand that when someone is trying to catch sorrow by the throat in the darkness and strangle it, a witness is not appreciated.

14

BHUPATI, AFTER HE WAS FREED FROM HIS NEWSPAPER, HAD painted a picture of the future in his mind. He had vowed not to get involved in any unrealisable aspirations, any futile ambitions, but with Charu, spend his days reading, loving, and fulfilling the everyday details of household duties. He had thought, those homely joys which are the most easily available yet so beautiful, that can be touched and lived everyday yet remain always pure and clear, with those simple joys he would light an evening lamp in the corner of his life's home and so begin to live a private peace. Talk and laughter, the everyday small arrangements for each other's delight and pleasure, all this does not require much effort, yet joy becomes abundant.

When he actually attempted this, he found simple joy was not so simple. If the things money can't buy are not naturally within one's reach, there is no other way of finding them.

Bhupati could not, in any way, make pleasant or delightful the times he spent with Charu. For this he blamed himself. He thought, 'After twelve years of newspaper work I have lost the art of conversing with my wife.' As soon as the evening lamp is lit, Bhupati enters the room with great eagerness—he says one or two words, Charu says one or two words, then Bhupati cannot think of anything more to say. Because of this incapacity he begins to feel embarrassed in front of Charu. He had thought that conversing with his wife would be so easy, yet for a fool like him it was this difficult. It was easier to make a speech at a formal gathering.

He had thought the evenings would be made beautiful with laughter, love and affection. Yet, living through those very evenings had become a problem for them. After a strained silence Bhupati thinks, 'I'll go.' But what will Charu think if he leaves? So he doesn't get up. He says, 'Charu, want to play cards?' Charu doesn't see any way out and says, 'Alright.' Reluctantly she brings the cards, makes terrible mistakes and so loses easily—no pleasure remains in the game.

Bhupati gave all this a great deal of thought and one day asked Charu, 'Charu, maybe we should bring Manda here. You're becoming very alone.'

Charu flared up as soon as she heard Manda's name.

She said, 'No, I don't need Manda.'

Bhupati laughed. Inside, he was pleased. A virtuous, devoted wife has no patience in the face of any lapses of devotion and virtue.

Steadying herself after the first attack of animosity, Charu thought that if Manda was here she could have kept Bhupati happy. The joy that Bhupati wanted from her she could not in any way give him, she felt this and was pained by it. Bhupati had left everything else in the world and was trying to extricate all his life's joy from Charu, she saw this single-minded effort and felt deeply the poverty of her inner self, she became alarmed. Why doesn't Bhupati resort to something else? Why doesn't he begin another newspaper? Till now, Charu had never had to cultivate the art of entertaining Bhupati, Bhupati had never demanded of her any looking after, never asked for any joys, he had not made Charu his life's greatest necessity; suddenly today he brings all his needs to her to be fulfilled, she cannot find anything to satisfy him. What Bhupati wants, what will fulfil him, Charu doesn't really know; even if she knows, it is not something which is easily in her power to give.

If Bhupati had advanced little by little, it would not have been so hard for Charu. But suddenly overnight Bhupati seemed to have become bankrupt and sat before her with an empty begging bowl. Charu did not know what to do.

Charu said, 'Alright, have Manda brought here. If she is here you will be well looked after.'

Bhupati laughed and said, 'Looking after? I don't need it.'

Bhupati thought, 'I am a very prosaic man, I just cannot keep Charu happy.'

Thinking this he began to read literature. Sometimes, when friends came to the house, they were surprised to find Bhupati with Tennyson, Byron or Bankim's stories. Seeing this untimely love of literature his friends began to ridicule him. Bhupati laughed and said, 'Well, even the bamboo tree flowers, but when it will flower no one knows.'

One day, Bhupati lit a large lamp in the bedroom. In the beginning he felt shy and hesitant; after a while he said, 'Should I read you something?'

Charu said, 'Why don't you?'

Bhupati: What shall I read?

Charu: Whatever you want.

Bhupati saw Charu's lack of eagerness and began to feel somewhat less enthusiastic. Even then he gathered courage and said, 'I'll translate something from Tennyson and read it to you.'

Charu said, 'Read.'

Everything was ruined. Hesitation and lack of enthusiasm interrupted the flow of his recitation, the correct Bengali translations did not come to him. Charu's empty gaze told him she wasn't paying attention. That lamp-lit, small room, that evening time's private leisure, did not fulfil itself.

Once or twice Bhupati again made this mistake and in the end abandoned the attempt to enjoy literature along with his wife.

15

When the body suffers a great injury, the nerves become numb, and in the beginning, no pain can be felt.

In the same way, Charu, at the onset of this separation, did not fully feel Amal's absence.

In the end, as the days began to go by, Amal's absence increased, by slow degrees, the emptiness of Charu's world. Charu is bewildered by this terrible discovery. Coming out of an arbour, what desert has she suddenly stepped into? Day after day goes by, and this vast expanse of arid land keeps stretching further and further. She knew nothing about this desert.

When she wakes in the morning, suddenly, her heart seems to contract—she remembers, Amal is not there. In the day, when she sits on the veranda to make paan, she keeps thinking, Amal will not come up and surprise her. Sometimes, absentmindedly, she makes too much paan, and immediately she remembers, there is no one to have all of it. Whenever she steps into the kitchen, the thought rises in her mind, Amal does not have to be given his food and tea. When she reaches the limits of the restless inner rooms of her self, something reminds her that Amal will not be returning from college as he used to. No new books, no new writings, no news, no fun and laughter can be looked forward to. There is no one for whom to sew, to write, to buy something beautiful.

Charu was bewildered by all the movement within her, by her own unbearable pain. It was a torment without rest. She asked herself constantly, 'Why? Why so much pain? What is Amal to me, that I should feel so much pain? What has happened to me? After so long, what is this that has happened to me? Maids, servants, even hawkers and labourers on the street walk by without a care, why did this happen to me? Oh God, why have you put me in such trouble?'

She keeps questioning herself and is astonished, but the pain does not subside. The memory of Amal surrounds her so completely, inside and outside, that it leaves no place for her to escape to.

Bhupati should have rescued her from this attack of memories, instead, he too, pained by the separation, loving fool that he is, keeps reminding her of Amal.

In the end, Charu gave up completely—she stopped fighting herself. She admitted defeat and accepted her situation without protest. With great care, she planted the memory of Amal in her heart.

Eventually things became like this. Charu's single-minded recollections of Amal became a source of pride for her—as if these memories were her life's true worth.

She decided on a particular time in between her household work. At that time, alone, with the door closed, she would search her memories for every incident in her life with Amal. Lying on the bed, with her face on a pillow, she would say, over and over, 'Amal, Amal, Amal.' From across the oceans there seemed to come the reply, 'Bouthan, what is it, Bouthan?' Charu would close her wet eyes and say, 'Amal, why did you leave me in anger? I didn't do anything wrong. If you had left in peace and joy I don't think I would be suffering so much.' Charu pronounced all her words as if Amal were right before her and said, 'Amal, I haven't forgotten you even for a day. Not for a day, not for a moment. All that is meaningful in my life you brought to blossom, my life's essence will be dedicated to your worship.'

In this way, Charu, beneath the landscape of all her household work, all her duties, dug an underground tunnel. In that lightness, motionless darkness, she built a secret temple of sorrow, decorated only with a garland of her tears. There, her husband, the rest of the world, had no right to enter. If that place was secret, it was also profound, also most beloved. At the door of this temple she abandoned all the disguises of the outer world and entered in her unveiled, true nature. When she came out she put the mask back on her face and returned to the arena of the world's talk, activities and laughter.

16

In this way, Charu gave up struggling with herself and found a kind of peace in the vastness of her grief and single-mindedly gave herself to the devotion and care of her husband. When Bhupati was asleep, Charu would slowly touch her head to his feet. In serving him, in her household work, she did not keep unfulfilled even his least desire. Bhupati was upset when the relatives they had sheltered or brought up were not well taken care of. Charu knew this and she saw to it that her hospitality towards them was always unfailing. In this way, after finishing all her household work, she would eat the remains of the food left by Bhupati on his plate, as if it were prasad, and so end her day.

Through this love and care of Charu's Bhupati seemed to acquire a new youth. It was as if he had not really married his wife before, after so long he seemed to be married to her. In the way he dressed, his laughter and his jesting, a new man appeared who pushed away the worries of the world to one side. After the ending of a disease hunger increases, the body consciously experiences once again the ability to enjoy things. In the same way, after so long, there came to Bhupati a new and overwhelming emotional life. Bhupati, hiding the fact from friends and even from Charu, began to read poetry. He thought, only with the going away of the paper and the coming of so much sorrow, after so long I have been able to rediscover my wife.

Bhupati said to Charu, 'Charu, why have you stopped writing completely?'

Charu said, 'As if there was anything great about my writing.'

Bhupati: But honestly, your writing is more original than any other contemporary writer of today. My opinion is exactly the same as *Vishwabandhu*'s.

Charu: Oh, stop it.

'Look,' said Bhupati, taking a volume of *Sarorohu*. He began comparing Amal and Charu's work. Charu, red-faced, snatched the volume from Bhupati's hands and hid it inside her anchal.

Bhupati thought to himself, it is hard to write unless one has a writing companion; I must work on my writing and then gradually I will be able to awaken Charu's enthusiasm again.

Bhupati very secretively took a notebook and began to write. Looking at the dictionary, scratching out what he had written, rewriting it, all of this filled up his unemployed days. It took so much effort, so much straining for him to write, that slowly he began to believe in these compositions that were the fruit of his hard labours and to feel towards them a tender affection.

In the end, Bhupati had his writing copied out in another's hand and took it to Charu. He said, 'A friend of mine has just started writing. I don't understand anything of all this, will you read it once and see how you like it?' Bhupati handed the notebook to Charu and walked away. Charu very easily saw through this simple trick of Bhupati's.

She read; noticing the style and the subject, she smiled a little. Charu was making so many arrangements in order to make complete her devotion to her husband, why was he, in such a juvenile way, scattering the offerings of her worship? Why did he want to gain Charu's admiration? If he did nothing, if he was not always trying to attract Charu's attention, then worshipping her husband would be simple and easy for Charu. Charu wanted very much that Bhupati, in no way, make himself smaller than her. Charu folded the notebook, leaned back on her pillow, stared far away and thought for a long time. Amal would also bring his new compositions to her.

In the evening, an eager Bhupati busied himself in observing the potted plants outside the bedroom, he did not have the courage to ask any questions.

Charu, of her own accord, said, 'Is this your friend's first attempt at writing?'

Bhupati said, 'Yes.'

Charu: This is wonderful. It doesn't seem like a first attempt.

Bhupati, extremely pleased, began to wonder how he could bring his own name to bear on the writings. Bhupati's notebook began to fill up with great rapidity. The author's name was also revealed without much delay.

17

Charu knew very well the days on which the mail came from abroad. At first, from Aden, there was a letter for Bhupati, in which Amal sent Charu his pranam; there was a letter from Suez for Bhupati, Charu was sent his pranam in that as well. A letter arrived from Malta. In it, the postscript contained a pranam for Charu.

Charu did not receive a single letter from Amal. She asked Bhupati for the letters he had received and read them over and over again—besides the pranam there was no mention of Charu anywhere.

Charu, over these last few days, had taken shelter under an awning of quiet, peaceful sorrow. Amal's indifference destroyed that shelter. Inside, her heart began to rend apart again. The stable world of her household duties was rocked once again by an earthquake.

Nowadays, Bhupati would sometimes wake in the middle of the night and find that Charu was not in bed. He would look for her, and find her sitting at the window of the southern room. Seeing him, Charu would quickly get up and say, 'It was hot in the bedroom today, so I came here to sit in the breeze.'

This made Bhupati anxious and he made arrangements for a fan in the bedroom and, fearing that Charu may be in precarious health, began to always keep an eye on her. Charu would smile and say, 'I am fine. Why are you getting needlessly anxious?' To bring about this smile she had to use the entire strength of her heart.

Amal reached England. Charu had decided that on the way he probably did not have enough of an opportunity to write to her separately, once he reached England he would send a long letter. But that long letter did not come.

On the days that the mail from England was supposed to arrive, beneath all her work and conversations Charu would be utterly restless. In case Bhupati said, 'There's no letter for you,' she could not gather enough courage to ask if there was.

On one such day Bhupati walked up to her very quietly and with a hint of a smile, said, 'I have something here. Want to see it?'

Charu, anxious, startled, said, 'Where? Show it to me.'

Bhupati did not want to show it to her yet. He wanted the fun to last a little longer.

Impatiently, Charu tried to grab the desired object from beneath Bhupati's shawl. She said to herself, 'Since the morning something has been telling me my letter will come—it cannot be in vain.'

Bhupati's sense of fun seemed to increase. Evading Charu, he began to move around the bed. Charu, in immense irritation, sat down on the bed with tears in her eyes.

Extremely pleased by Charu's overwhelming eagerness, Bhupati brought out from beneath his shawl the notebook in which he had composed his writings and, hastily putting it in Charu's lap, said, 'Don't get angry. Here, take it.'

18

Though Amal had let Bhupati know that his studies would keep him busy and for a long time he wouldn't be able to write home, even then when the mail brought no letters from him, the whole world, for Charu, became a bed of thorns.

In the middle of an evening conversation, Charu, in an almost aloof way, in a quiet voice, asked her husband, 'Look, can't a telegram be sent to England to find out how Amal is?'

Bhupati said, 'We got a letter from him two weeks ago, he is busy now with his studies.'

Charu: Oh, then there's no need. I thought, he's abroad, he may have fallen ill—one never knows.

Bhupati: No, if he was ill we would know. And it is quite expensive to send a telegram.

Charu: Really? I thought, at the most it would cost one or two rupees.

Bhupati: What are you saying? It is almost one hundred rupees.

Charu: In that case it really is out of the question.

After a day or two Charu said to Bhupati, 'My sister is in Chinsurah right now, will you go there today and find out how she is?'

Bhupati: Why, is she ill?

Charu: No, she's not ill. You know how happy they always are to see you.

At Charu's request Bhupati got into his carriage and rode towards Howrah station. On his way there was a line of bullock carts and his carriage had to stop to let them pass. While he was waiting, the regular telegram man saw Bhupati and handed him a telegram. When he saw it was a telegram from England Bhupati became apprehensive. He thought, perhaps Amal is ill. With rising uneasiness he opened the telegram. It said, 'I am well.'

What did this mean? He examined the telegram and saw that it was the reply to a prepaid one already sent from Calcutta.

Bhupati did not go to Howrah. He turned his carriage around, came home, and handed his wife the telegram. Charu's face paled at seeing the telegram in Bhupati's hands.

Bhupati said, 'I don't understand the meaning of this.' After asking a few questions Bhupati understood. Charu had pawned her own jewellery to borrow money and pay for the telegram.

Bhupati thought, there was no need to do so much. If she had asked me I would have sent it myself. To send the servant, secretly, and have her jewellery pawned—this was not a good thing.

Every once in a while the question rose in Bhupati's mind, why did Charu have to be so excessive about it? A vague suspicion began imperceptibly to force its way into him. This suspicion Bhupati did not want to look at directly, he tried to let it remain forgotten, but its pain did not leave him.

19

Amal is in good health, yet he does not write. How did this complete and terrible break come about? Charu wants to ask Amal this question and receive an answer, face to face, but there is an ocean in between—and no way to cross it. Cruel separation, helpless separation, beyond all questions, beyond all redress, separation.

Charu can barely keep herself going. Work is left incomplete, in everything mistakes are made, the servants steal; people see sharply her wretchedness and they talk, they spread rumours, Charu is not aware of any of this. This is how things became. Charu would be suddenly startled; in the middle of a conversation she would get up and go away to cry; the very mention of Amal's name would make her face pale.

In the end even Bhupati saw everything and what he had never imagined even for a moment he realised now—the world became to him completely old, withered, worn out.

Till now he had been deluded by the awakening of a new joy. The memories of those past days now began to embarrass him. Should the inexperienced who doesn't know precious gems be deceived in this way by any ordinary stone? All of Charu's words of love, her indulgences, came back at him, calling him an ignorant fool and whipping him as if with a cane.

In the end, when he remembered his writings, composed with so much effort, so much care, Bhupati, like someone goaded from behind, went to Charu and said, 'Where are my writings?'

Charu said, 'They're still with me.'

Bhupati said, 'Give them to me.'

Charu was frying kachuris for Bhupati. She said, 'Do you need them right now?'

Bhupati said, 'Yes, right now.'

Charu took the frying pan off the fire and brought out the papers from her cupboard. Impatiently, Bhupati took all the papers from her hands and threw them into the fire. Charu anxiously tried to take them out, saying, 'What is this you've done?'

Bhupati grasped her hand and shouted, 'Let it be.'

Charu stood there astonished. All the writings were burnt to ashes. Charu understood. She took a deep breath. She let the frying be and slowly walked away.

Bhupati had not planned to destroy his papers in front of Charu. But the fire was right there, and when he saw it the blood seemed to rise inside him. Bhupati lost his self control.

All the efforts of the deceived were thrown into the fire before the deceiver herself.

Everything turned to ashes and when Bhupati's sudden impetuosity was calmed then Charu, bearing the burden of her own crime, in deep sorrow, silently walked away, her head bowed. Bhupati saw this and something awakened within him—he looked before him and saw, Charu had been cooking, with her own hands, with care, something that he loved.

Bhupati stood, leaning on the railing of the balcony. He thought—all this tireless effort of Charu's, all this intensity of deception, was there anything more poignant than this in the whole world? All this guile was not the mere, lowly deception of a deceiver; to be able to deceive, this woman abandoned by fate, had to bear an even greater sharpening of the pain and torment inside her, and every day, every moment, wrench out these deceptions as if from her heart's blood. Bhupati said to himself, helpless woman, grieving woman. There was no need for this, I did not need any of this. For so long I was not loved yet I did not know what not-love was—I carried on well by merely checking proofs, writing articles—I did not need all this to be done for me.

Then he removed his own life far from Charu's life—the way a doctor looks at a patient with a terrible disease. Bhupati looked at Charu in the same way, as if he did not have any relationship with her. This helpless woman, she has been besieged in all directions by an indomitable world. There is no one to whom she can tell everything, it is not something that can be told, there is no place where she can lay bare her heart and weep—but this inexpressible, inevitable, irredeemable, everyday piling up weight of pain, she has to carry, and like an ordinary person, like her peaceful neighbours, she has to do her everyday household work.

Bhupati went to the bedroom and saw—Charu stood holding the bars of the window, looking out with tearless, unblinking eyes. Bhupati slowly, slowly, came and stood near her—he didn't speak, he put his hand on her head.

20

Friends asked Bhupati, 'What is it? Why so busy?'

'A newspaper,' said Bhupati.

'Once again a newspaper? Do you want to wrap everything you have in a newspaper and throw it away into the Ganga?'

'No. Not my own paper again.'

'Then?'

'There will be a paper published from Mysore. They've made me the editor.'

'Leaving everything to go to Mysore? Are you taking Charu with you?'

'No, my uncles will come and stay here with her.'

'Editorship is like an intoxication for you.'

'A man needs at least one thing to be intoxicated by.'

At leaving time, Charu asked, 'When will you come back?'

Bhupati said, 'If you feel alone, write to me, I'll come.'

He said this and walked towards the door. Charu ran up to him and grasped his hand. She said, 'Take me with you. Don't leave me here.'

Bhupati stopped. He stood there, looking at Charu's face. Charu's grasp loosened and his hand came away. He moved, away from Charu and out onto the veranda.

The flames of Amal's absence, the memory of him, had completely surrounded the house and Charu, like a doe engulfed by a forest fire, was trying to leave the house behind her. But, he thought, didn't she, even once, think about me? Where will I escape to? A wife who is every day absorbed in the thought of someone else, will I not even be given the chance to go away and forget her? Will I have to be with her every day even in that silent, friendless exile of Mysore? After a whole day's hard work when I come home in the evening, then how unbearable the evening will be with this still and sorrowful woman. How long can I hold her close to my heart, this woman with a dead weight inside her? How many years longer will I have to live like this, day after day? The shelter that is broken and in pieces, can't I throw away its broken bricks and wood? Do I have to carry their weight on my shoulders wherever I go?

Bhupati came in and said to Charu, 'No. I can't do that.'

All the blood drained away from Charu's face, leaving it as dry and white as paper. She clutched the edge of the bed.

Instantly, Bhupati said, 'Come, Charu. Come with me.'

Charu said, 'No. Let it be.'

THE GHAT'S TALE

If events were etched in stone, you would have been able to read the tales of many ages on my steps. If you want to hear about the past then sit on this step of mine; listen attentively to the sound of the water; you will be able to hear so many forgotten tales from long ago.

I remember a day exactly like this one. There are a few days left till the month of Ashwin. At dawn, a light, sweet, new winter breeze is bringing renewed life into the limbs of one who has just awakened. The trees and leaves, in the same way, are shivering a little.

The Ganga is full. Only four of my steps are above water. Water and land seem to have merged into one another. On the shore, the water has reached the foot of the mango tree where an undergrowth of taro has sprung up. Near that bend of the river three ancient stacks of bricks can be seen above the water. The fishermen's boats that were tied to the foot of the babul tree are floating and swaying on the waters of the morning tide—the restless, youthful tidal waters are playfully attacking them from both sides, as if tweaking their ears and shaking them in fun and gentle laughter.

The light that is falling on the swollen river is the colour of molten gold, the colour of the champa flower. There is no other time when the sunlight has this colour. It falls on the sandbank, on its fields of kaash. The kaash flowers have not all bloomed yet, they have just begun blooming.

The fishermen untie their boats, saying 'Ram, Ram'. The way birds spread their wings in the light and fly with joy in the blue sky, in the same way, these small boats with their small swollen sails are out in the sunlight. They seem like birds; they float on the water like swans, but spread their wings in the sky with delight.

Bhattacharya mahashaya has come at his regular time, with his kosha-kushi, for a bath. One or two women have begun arriving to collect water.

It was not very long ago. You might feel it is a long time. But I feel it happened only the other day. My days are as the waves on the Ganga, they toss and float away, and through the ages I watch in silence—so time seems short for me. For me the light of day and the shadows of night are cast daily upon the Ganga, and are every day wiped away—they never leave an impression. So, even though I look old, my heart is forever young. The algae of years of memories has not covered me so as to keep out the rays of the sun. Sometimes, by chance an algae floats in and clings to my sides, then it is once again carried away by the waves. But I cannot say there is nothing that has stayed. Where the waves of the Ganga do not reach, there, in my crevices, have sprung up creepers and weeds and moss; they are witnesses to my past, it is they who have held the past in their loving embrace and kept it forever green and tender, forever new. The Ganga recedes from me every day, step by step, and I too, step by step, grow older.

That old woman from the Chakrabarti house, who has had her bath and is shivering under her namabali as she counts her prayer beads while she returns home; her mother's mother was then a little girl. I remember she played a game. Every day she would set an aloe leaf afloat on the water; there was an eddy on my left side, there the leaf would swirl around, and she would put down her water pitcher and keep looking at it; when I looked again, some time later, she had become a woman and brought her own daughter along to fill water, that daughter too grew up, and when the little girls splashed water on each other she rebuked them and taught them good manners, then I would remember the aloe leaf boat with amusement.

The story that I want to tell doesn't seem to come easily. As I begin one tale, the water's flow brings along another one. Stories come, stories go, I can't hold on to them. Only some tales, like the aloe leaf, get caught in an eddy and keep coming back. So a tale keeps coming around to me with its load of wares, who knows when it might sink. Like the leaf it is very small, there is nothing much in it, perhaps two flowers to play with. If she sees it sink, a tender-hearted young girl will only sigh and return home.

There, next to the temple, where you see the fence of the Goshai's cowshed, used to be a babul tree. Under that there was a weekly market. The Goshais had not begun living here yet. Where they now have their family shrine there was only a leaf-thatched shelter.

This peepal tree which today has spread its branches through my ribs, and like a monstrous, elongated, hard net of fingers has clutched in its fist my cracked stone heart, this tree was then only a tiny sapling. It was growing and raising its head with its tiny leaves. In the sunlight, the shadows of its leaves would play over me all day, its new roots would play near my heart like a child's fingers. If anyone tore off a single leaf, it would hurt me.

Even though I was quite old, I was still straight in those days. Today my spine is broken and I am as bent and crooked as a deformed person, with cracks in hundreds of places and in my hollows numerous frogs prepare for their long winter sleep. In those days, I was not in this state. Only on my left side there were two bricks missing; in that hollow a drongo had made its nest. At dawn, when the drongo began to wake with rustling sounds and move its tail, forked like that of a fish, up and down a few times, and then whistling, fly away into the sky, then I knew it was time for Kusum to arrive at the riverbank.

The girl whom I am speaking of was called Kusum by the other girls. When Kusum's small shadow fell on the water I used to wish I could capture that shadow, could bind that shadow in my stone—that was the kind of sweetness she had. When she stepped onto my stone, her fourfold anklets tinkling, the creepers and weeds and moss seemed to be filled with joy. It is not that Kusum played a lot, or talked or joked very much, but what was surprising is that she had more companions than anyone else. All the naughtiest girls couldn't do without her. Some used to call her 'Kushi', some 'Khushi', others 'Rakkushi'. Her mother called her 'Kusmi'. Often I used to see her sitting by the water. In her heart there was a special affinity with this water. She loved the water very much.

After some time I did not see Kusum. Bhuvan and Swarna used to come to the bank and weep. I heard that their 'Kushi, Khushi, Rakkushi' had been taken to her husband's home. I heard that where she had been taken there was no Ganga. In that place there were strangers, new homes, new streets and roads. Someone had taken away the lotus from the water to plant it on land.

Eventually I have forgotten all about Kusum. A year has passed. The girls at the riverbank no longer talk much about her. One evening I feel the touch of very familiar footsteps and am suddenly surprised. It seems like Kusum's footsteps. They are, but there are no anklets tinkling any more. The feet do not have the same music. I have always experienced the touch of Kusum's feet and the sound of her anklets together—today not hearing the sound of the anklets, the waves of the evening water begin to sound despondent; in the mango grove the wind rustles the leaves and makes a sound like a lament.

Kusum has become a widow. I heard that her husband used to work abroad; she had only met him once or twice. Informed of her widowhood by a letter, having wiped off her sindoor when she was eight years old, having taken off all her jewellery, she has returned again to her land near the Ganga. But most of her friends are no longer here. Bhuvan, Swarna and Amala have all gone to their husbands' homes. Only Sharat remains, but I hear she too will be married in the month of Aghran. Kusum is very alone. But, when she used to put her head on her knees and sit quietly on my steps I used to feel as if the waves of the river were raising their hands together and calling to her, 'Kushi, Khushi, Rakkushi.'

The way that the Ganga swells before one's eyes at the onset of the monsoons, in the same way Kusum every day became more full of beauty and youth. But her faded clothes, her sad face and her quiet nature cast a shadow that covered that youth, that manifest beauty, so that an ordinary person did not notice it. It was as if no one could see that Kusum had grown into a young woman. I could not. I have never seen her as older than that little girl. She no longer wore anklets but when she walked I could hear those anklets tinkling. How ten years passed in this way the people of the village did not care to know.

That year, at the end of the month of Bhadra, there came a day like this one. Your great grandmothers woke that morning and saw exactly this kind of gentle sunlight. When, with their long veils covering their faces and their pitchers in their arms, they made their way through the trees and plants over the uneven paths of the village to make the morning light over me even more bright, talking to each other all the way, then even the possibility of your existence had not entered a corner of their minds. The way that you cannot imagine that even your grandmothers played as children, the way that this day is a truth, is alive, those days too were true, with young hearts like yours they swayed between joy and sorrow, in that same way this winter's day—without them, without even a remnant of the memories of their joys and sorrows, today's joyous picture of a day glowing with the winter sun—that is something that was unknown to them even in their imagination.

On that day the beginnings of the north wind came in little by little from dawn and made a few babul flowers fall on me. On my stone there were a few streaks of dew. That morning a young, tall, fair-skinned sanyasi with a calm, radiant face came and took shelter in the Shiva temple before me. The news of the sanyasi's arrival spread through the village. The women kept their pitchers aside and crowded the temple to pay their respects to him.

Every day the crowd grew. In the first place he was a sanyasi, moreover he was incomparably handsome, and above all he never neglected anyone, took the children on his lap, and asked the women about their household work. Among the women he was very rapidly given an important place. Many men also came to him. Some days he would recite the Bhagavat, some days expound the Bhagavad Gita, some days discuss a particular shastra. Some people would come to him for advice, others for a mantra. Some would come for medicines. The women would come to the ghat and say to each other—oh, how handsome. It seemed as if Mahadeva had himself come to dwell in his temple.

Every day at dawn, just before sunrise, when the sanyasi stood in the water facing the morning star and in a slow, grave voice sang hymns to the dawn, then I could not hear the sound of the water. Every day, while listening to his voice the sky on the east became blood-red, next to the clouds there appeared streaks of sunlight, the darkness would fall away like the burst calyx of a blossoming bud, and the red flower of the morning would bloom little by little in the lake of the sky. I used to think, this great man stands in the waters of the Ganga, looks eastward and says a great prayer, and as he utters each word the night's magic is dispelled, the moon and stars set in the west, the sun begins to rise in the east, and the aspect of the world is transformed. Who was this conjurer? After his bath, when the sanyasi rose with his tall, fair body like the high flame of a sacrificial fire, water dripped from his matted locks, and the first rays of the sun fell all over his body and seemed to be reflected from it.

In this way a few more months passed. In the month of Chaitra, at the time of the solar eclipse, many people came to bathe in the Ganga. There was a huge market below the babul tree. On this occasion people also came to see the sanyasi. Many women had come from the village where Kusum's husband's family lived.

In the morning, as the sanyasi was sitting on my step and saying his prayers, a woman saw him and said to her companion, 'That is Kusum's husband!'

Someone else shifted her veil with two fingers and said, 'Oh my, you're right. He is the youngest son of the Chatterjis.'

Another woman, who was not concerned about her veil, said, 'Ah, the same forehead, the same nose, the same eyes.'

Yet another did not really even look at the sanyasi, let out a sigh, and pushing her pitcher against the water, said, 'Ah, can he still be alive? Will he ever come back? Is Kusum so fortunate?'

Then someone said, 'He didn't have such a thick beard.'

Someone said, 'He wasn't so thin.' Someone said, 'He isn't so tall.'

In this way the matter was settled and was not brought up again. Everyone in the village had seen the sanyasi except Kusum. There were too many people here and so Kusum had stopped coming to me. One evening, seeing the full moon rise, she must have remembered our old relationship.

At that time there was no one else at the riverbank. The cicadas were calling. The temple bell had stopped ringing a little while ago, and the last waves of sound became fainter and fainter and disappeared like a shadow in the forests on the opposite bank. There is bright moonlight. The waters of the tide are lapping at the shore. Kusum sits, throwing a shadow on me. Before her, on the breast of the Ganga is the unrestricted, expansive moonlight—behind her in the trees and bushes, in the shadow of the temple, in the foundations of a ruined house, near the pond, in the forest of tal trees, the darkness hides, its body and face covered. Bats hang from the branches of the chatim tree. An owl sits on the spire of the temple and cries out as though it were weeping. Near the village dwellings the jackals' howls rise sharply and then stop.

The sanyasi came out slowly from the temple. He came to the ghat, walked down one or two steps, and seeing a woman alone was about to turn back, when Kusum turned and looked behind her.

The sari fell back from around her head. The moonlight fell on Kusum's face as if on an upturned flower. In that moment the two saw each other. It was as if they came to know each other. It seemed as though they had known each other in a previous life.

An owl screeched overhead and flew away. The sound brought her back to her senses and she raised the end of her sari over her head. She got up, fell on the ground and touched the sanyasi's feet.

The sanyasi blessed her and asked, 'What is your name?'

Kusum said, 'My name is Kusum.'

They did not speak any more that night. Kusum lived nearby, and she slowly went home. That night the sanyasi sat for a long time on my steps. In the end, when the moon had come from the east to the west, he rose and went back into the temple.

From the day after that I would see Kusum coming every day and touching the sanyasi's feet. When the sanyasi explained the shastras she stood on one side and listened. After completing his morning prayers the sanyasi called Kusum and spoke to her of dharma. How could she understand everything he said? But she listened to it with great attention; she did whatever the sanyasi told her. Every day she worked at the temple, was not lazy about serving God, picked flowers for the puja, and brought water from the Ganga to clean the temple.

Kusum sat on my steps and thought about everything the sanyasi told her. Slowly, her sight seemed to expand, her heart seemed to open. She began to see what she had never seen, to hear what she had never heard. The dark shadow that had lain over her serene face disappeared. When she fell at the sanyasi's feet in the morning, filled with devotion, she looked like a dew-washed flower to be offered to the deity. A pure joy made her whole body glow.

At this time, when the winter is nearing its end, a winter wind blows, and on some days suddenly in the evening a spring wind comes from the south, and the chill in the sky seems entirely gone—after a long time a flute can be heard in the village, and the sound of singing. The fishermen let their boats run free on the current, keep aside their oars and sing songs about Krishna. From the branches the birds suddenly begin calling to each other in great delight. This is the kind of time that has come now.

The spring breeze has touched my stone heart and little by little infused it with youthfulness; it seems that my creepers and leaves have drawn from this new, youthful effervescence in my heart and have bloomed with flowers. Now I do not see Kusum any more. For a while she has not come to the temple, or the riverbank, and she is not seen with the sanyasi.

I do not know what happened in the meantime. After some time, Kusum and the sanyasi met on my steps.

Kusum bent her head and said, 'Master, did you send for me?'

'Yes. Why don't I see you any more? Why such neglect nowadays towards serving God?'

Kusum was quiet.

'Tell me what is on your mind.'

Kusum turned her face away a little and said, 'Master, I am a sinner, so the neglect.'

With tremendous love in his voice the sanyasi said, 'Kusum, I can tell that your heart is unquiet.'

Kusum started—perhaps she wondered how much the sanyasi had understood. Her eyes began to fill with tears and she sat down where she stood; she covered her face with the end of her sari and began crying at the sanyasi's feet.

The sanyasi moved away a bit and said, 'Tell me clearly what is disturbing you, and I will show you a way to peace.'

She began speaking in a voice of unwavering devotion, but she paused sometimes, and at other times words failed her—'If you command it, I will certainly tell you. But I cannot say it well, and I feel in your heart you know everything. Master, I used to revere someone like a God, I used to worship him, and that joy had filled my heart. But one night I had a dream, in which he was the lord of my heart; somewhere in a bakul grove he had taken my right hand in his left and was speaking to me words of love. I did not think this to be impossible, or surprising. I awoke from my dream, but not the feeling that the dream left behind. When I saw this person the next day, I did not see him as I had before. I kept seeing the image from my dream. I fled far away in fear, but the image stayed with me. Since then the restlessness in my heart cannot be stilled; everything is darkness.'

When Kusum was saying these words and wiping her tears, I felt the sanyasi press his right foot down on my stone with all his strength.

When Kusum finished he said, 'You have to tell me who you saw in your dream.'

Kusum folded her hands together and said, 'I cannot tell you that.'

The sanyasi said, 'I am asking you for your own good, tell me clearly who he is.'

Kusum wrung her two hands violently, then folded them and said, 'Do I have to tell you?'

The sanyasi said, 'Yes, you have to.' Kusum immediately said, 'Master, it is you.'

As soon as her own terrible words reached her own ears she collapsed on my hard lap. The sanyasi remained standing like a stone image.

When Kusum came to consciousness the sanyasi said slowly, 'You have obeyed my every word; I will say one thing more, and you must obey. I will leave here today; we will not meet again. You have to forget me. Tell me you will strive to do so.'

Kusum stood up, looked at the sanyasi's face and said slowly, 'Master, it will be done.'

The sanyasi said, 'Then I am leaving.'

Kusum did not say anything else, she touched his feet, and took the dust of his feet onto her head. The sanyasi left.

Kusum said, 'He has ordered me to forget him.' Then she walked slowly down into the waters of the Ganga.

She has spent so much time near this water ever since her childhood; when she was exhausted if the water did not reach out and take her in its arms, who else would? The moon set, the night became utterly dark. I heard the sound of a splash in the water, but could not make out anything else. In the darkness the wind began to rise; as if it wanted to blow out the stars in case even the tiniest thing could be seen.

The one who used to play in my lap has today finished playing and moved away, I don't know where.

NOTEBOOK

As soon as she learnt to write, Uma became a source of great trouble. In every room, on every wall, she draws unsteady lines and writes with coal in large, unformed letters: the rain falls, the leaves move.

She finds a copy of *Haridas's Secrets* under her sister-in-law's pillow, and writes on its pages with pencil: black water, red flower.

With her large lettered handwriting, she has obliterated most of the auspicious dates in the new almanac kept for the family's everyday use.

In her father's daily accounts book, she has written in the midst of the debit and credit: the one who studies is the one who rides a horse and carriage.

Till now, these literary pursuits did not face any obstacles, but in the end a grave disaster took place.

Uma's brother Gobindalal looked extremely harmless, but he often wrote for the newspapers. Listening to him talk, neither his family nor his neighbours would suspect him of being a thoughtful man. And in reality one cannot accuse him of thinking about anything at any time, but he writes; and his opinions are exactly the same as the majority of Bengal's readers.

There were some grave misconceptions among the European scientific community about physiology. Without the help of any kind of logic, using an exaggerated, energetic language, he wrote an essay demolishing these misconceptions.

One day, in the silent afternoon, Uma took her brother's pen and ink, and wrote on this essay—Gopal is a very good boy, he eats whatever he is given.

I don't believe that Uma had meant Gopal to symbolise the readers of the essay, but her brother's rage was limitless. At first he beat her, and in the end he took away her stub of a pencil, and a blunt ink-stained pen, snatching from her a carefully collected, meagre store of writing tools. The humiliated child, unable to completely understand the reason for such grave punishment, sat in a corner and wept with a wounded heart.

After the period of punishment was over, Gobindalal, with some contrition, returned her things, and over and above that, by giving her a bound and ruled notebook, tried to take away the little girl's grief.

Uma was then seven years old. From then on, this notebook was under her pillow at night, and in the day in her arm or lap.

When she went to the girls' school in the village, her hair in two little plaits, accompanied by her maid, the notebook went with her. Seeing it, some of the other girls were filled with wonder, some with greed, some with envy.

In the first year, she writes very carefully in the notebook—the birds are singing, the night is over. She would sit on the floor in the bedroom and holding the notebook she would read loudly and write. In this way she built up a collection of prose and poetry.

In the second year one or two independent compositions begin to make their appearance, very brief but filled with a pregnant meaning, and without introduction or conclusion. Here are a few examples.

Below where she had copied out the tale of the tiger and the heron from the *Kathamala,* there is a line which is not to be found in the *Kathamala* or anywhere in contemporary Bengali literature before this. The line is—I love Jashi very much.

No one should think that I am now about to tell a love story. Jashi is not an eleven or twelve year old boy in the neighbourhood. She is an old maidservant of the family, her real name is Jashoda.

But from this one cannot get definite proof of the little girl's feelings towards Jashi. Whoever may want to write a believable history of this matter, he will find in this very notebook, after two pages, a clear refutation of the earlier words.

Not only in one or two places, but in almost every instance one can observe Uma's tendency towards contradicting herself. In one place there are the words—I will never speak to Hari again in my life. (Not Haricharan, a boy, but Haridasi, a little girl who was her schoolmate.) Very soon after this there are words that make one believe that she has no closer friend in the three worlds than Hari.

The year after this, when Uma was nine, one morning a shehnai could be heard in the house. Uma was getting married. The groom's name was Pyarimohan. He was a literary associate of Gobindalal's. Although he was not very old, and had received a little bit of education, new ways of thought had not been able to penetrate his mind. For this the neighbours held him in high regard, and Gobindalal tried to follow his example, but was not entirely successful.

Uma, wearing a Benarasi sari, her tiny face hidden behind a veil, went weeping to her in-laws' house. Her mother told her, 'Darling, listen to your mother-in-law, do the housework, don't spend all your time reading and writing.'

Gobindalal said, 'Be careful, don't go about writing on the walls there; it isn't that kind of house. And don't you dare write on any of Pyarimohan's work.'

The little girl's heart began to tremble. She then realised that no one would make allowances for her where she was going; and what they considered a fault, an offence, a shortcoming, she would have to learn from many reprimands suffered over many days.

That morning too the shenai was playing. But it was doubtful whether there was anyone in that gathering of people who understood what was going on in the little girl's trembling heart covered by a veil, and jewels, and a Benaras sari.

Jashi also went with Uma. She was supposed to stay a few days, settle Uma into her in-laws' home and return. The loving Jashi, after much thought, had brought along Uma's notebook. This notebook was a fragment of her father's home; a loving memory of the brief time spent in the house where she was born; in crooked, unformed letters it told the brief story of her parents' love and care.

Into her untimely housewife's role it brought the sweet and tender hint of a young girl's freedom.

She did not write anything for a while after reaching her in-laws' house, she did not have the time. In the end, Jashi returned home.

That afternoon, she closed her bedroom door and, taking the notebook out of a tin box, weeping, she wrote—Jashi has gone home, I also want to go back to mother.

These days there is no time to copy things from *Charupath* and *Bodhoday*, there is also probably not much desire to do so. Therefore, there are no large gaps between the little girl's brief compositions. After the above-mentioned line there are these words—if Dada takes me home once then I will never destroy his writings again.

One hears that Uma's father often makes efforts to bring Uma home. But Gobindalal joins with Pyarimohan to oppose it.

Gobindalal says, now is the time for Uma to learn devotion to her husband, so if she is brought every so often to her parents' house, back into the love of her parents, her mind will be unnecessarily distracted. He wrote such a wonderful essay on this subject, combining advice and mockery, that no like-minded reader could keep himself from agreeing with the undeniable truth of his argument.

Having heard people talk about this Uma wrote in her notebook—Dada, I fall at your feet, take me back once to your house, I will never make you angry again.

One day Uma had shut the door and was writing something as insignificant and meaningless. Her sister-in-law Tilakmanjari became very curious. She thought, I want to see what she does with the door closed once in a while. Through a crack in the door she saw Uma writing. She was amazed. The goddess of learning, Saraswati, had never entered the inner rooms of their house in such a secret way.

Her younger sister Kanakmanjari also came and had a look.

The one younger than that, Anangamanjari, even she, raising herself on her toes with great difficulty, looked through the crack and penetrated the mystery of the closed room.

Uma, while writing, suddenly heard three familiar voices laughing outside. She understood what was happening, and very embarrassed, hid her face and kept lying on the bed.

Pyarimohan became worried when he heard this. If reading and writing began then novels and plays would be acquired and it would be hard to preserve the household's virtues.

Besides, he had, with great thought, built up a very subtle philosophy about this. He used to say, the power of the male and the power of the female together produced the power of the conjugal relationship, but if the power of the female was vanquished through education, the power of the male would become paramount. Then, male power would clash with male power to produce such a terrible destructive energy that the conjugal bond would be completely destroyed and the woman would become a widow. Till today, no one has been able to refute this theory.

Pyarimohan returned in the evening and remonstrated Uma roundly, and laughed at her as well. He said, 'We'll have to order a lawyer's turban, my wife will go to office with a pen tucked behind her ear.'

Uma didn't quite understand. She had not yet read Pyarimohan's essay, so she couldn't appreciate such wit. But inside, she shrank in remorse; she felt if the earth opened only then she could hide her shame by disappearing into its depths.

She didn't write for a long time. But one winter morning a beggar woman was singing an agamani song. Uma was resting her face against the bars of the window and listening quietly. As it is, in the winter sunlight all the memories of childhood return, over and above that, hearing an agamani song she could no longer restrain herself.

Uma could not sing. But ever since she had learnt to write she had the habit of writing down any song she heard. This took away the regret she felt at her own inability to sing. Today the beggar woman was singing:

The neighbours say to Uma's mother,
Your lost star has returned.
At this, the queen, almost crazed, comes running,
Where is Uma, tell me, where?
Weeping, the queen says, my Uma you've come,
Come to me my darling, come to me my darling,
Come to me my darling, let me hold you in my lap.
Instantly Uma stretches out her arms and puts them
Around her mother's neck,

Weeping with hurt pride she tells the queen,
Why didn't you come to fetch your daughter?

A hurtful pride filled Uma's heart, and her eyes brimmed with tears. Secretly she called the woman in and shut the door and began to write the song in her notebook.

Tilakmanjari, Kanakmanjari and Anangamanjari saw everything through that crack in the door and, clapping their hands, said, 'Boudidi, we can see everything you're doing.'

Uma immediately opened the door and came out and pleaded, 'Please, my darlings, don't tell anyone, I fall at your feet—I won't do it again, I won't write again.'

In the end Uma saw that Tilakmanjari was eyeing her notebook. Then she ran and clasped the notebook, to her chest. The sisters-in-law tried with a lot of force to snatch it away. Failing, Ananga went and called their brother.

Pyarimohan came and sat on the bed. In a thunderous voice he said, 'Give me the notebook. Seeing that his orders were not being obeyed he lowered his voice a few registers and said, 'Give it to me.'

The girl clasped the notebook to her chest and looked at her husband's face in utter supplication. When she saw that Pyarimohan had got up to snatch the notebook she threw it on the ground and fell on the floor, covering her face with her arms.

Pyarimohan took the notebook and began to read the little girl's writings out loud; hearing this Uma clasped the earth in a tighter embrace, and the three listeners were beside themselves with laughter.

Since then Uma has never got back her notebook.

Pyarimohan also had an exercise book, filled with essays expounding his subtle theories. But there was no benefactor of mankind to snatch *that* notebook away.

POSTMASTER

As soon as he began his first job, the postmaster was sent to the village of Ulapur. It was an insignificant village. There was an indigo planter's house nearby, and the sahib had made a lot of effort to get this new post office established there.

Our postmaster is a young man from Calcutta. Having arrived in this village the postmaster felt rather like a fish that has been brought out of the water and left on dry land. His office is in a dark thatched shed; not far away there is a weed-filled pond and on its borders, a jungle. The agent and the workers at the plantation have almost no leisure and they are not fit company for a gentleman.

Moreover, a young man from Calcutta does not know how to meet and mingle with people different from him. When he visits an unfamiliar place he becomes either arrogant or awkward. This is why he cannot mingle with the local residents. Yet he does not have much work on his hands. Sometimes he tries to write a poem or two. In the poems he expresses emotions which make it seem that his day is spent in great happiness, watching the trembling leaves and the clouds in the sky—but the lord of the inner self knows that if from an Arab tale a genie appeared and overnight cut down the leaves and branches and made tarred roads, and if tall buildings were to block the sight of clouds in the sky, then this half-dead progeny of the bhadralok world would receive a new lease of life.

The postmaster's salary is meagre. He has to cook his meals himself and a little orphan girl from the village does the rest of his work; in return she gets something to eat. The girl's name is Ratan. She is about twelve or thirteen years old. There is not much possibility of her getting married.

In the evening, when smoke rose, twisted and coiling, from the cowsheds in the village, crickets called in the bushes, in a distant village a group of always intoxicated bauls played their drums and cymbals and began to sing at the top of their voices—when, sitting on the dark porch watching the trees move, even a poet's heart would tremble a little—at such a time the postmaster would light a feeble lamp in one corner of the room and call, 'Ratan!' Ratan would sit near the door and wait for this call but would not enter the room immediately; she would say, 'What is it, Babu, why are you calling me?'

Postmaster: What are you doing?

Ratan: I was just going to light the fire for the stove—in the kitchen—

Postmaster: You can do your kitchen work later. Now get my hookah ready.

Without any delay Ratan would enter the room, her cheeks swelling as she blew on the hookah. Taking the hookah in his hands the postmaster would ask suddenly, 'Ratan, do you remember your mother?' There was much to say, she remembers some things and not others. Her father used to love her more than her mother, she remembers her father a little. After a hard day her father would return home in the evening; a few of those evenings are sketched clearly in her mind. As they talked Ratan would gradually sit down on the ground, at the postmaster's feet. She would remember she had a younger brother—on a monsoon day a long time ago they had pretended to be fishing in a pool with a line made from a broken branch—more than other important events it was this which kept returning to her mind. Sometimes as they talked it would become late and the postmaster felt too lazy to cook. There would be some leftovers from lunch and Ratan would quickly light the fire and make some rotis—they would both make do with that for dinner.

Sometimes in the evening, sitting on the office bench in the large shed, the postmaster would talk about his own home as well—about his younger brother, mother and elder sister, those for whom his heart ached while he sat alone in a foreign place. The things that always were on his mind but could not be mentioned to the workers in the plantation, he told a little illiterate girl, and it did not seem in the least strange. In the end the little girl began to refer to the postmaster's family as 'Ma, Didi, Dada', as if she had known them all her life. She had even built up an image of them in her child's heart.

One monsoon day, on an afternoon free of clouds, a somewhat warm and gentle wind began to blow; a fragrance arose from the wet grass and trees in the sunlight; it felt as if a tired earth's warm breath was touching the body; and somewhere, all afternoon, in nature's court, an insistent bird was making its complaint, over and over, in one long-drawn-out, sad note. The postmaster had no work on his hands—the movement of that day's rain-washed, smooth, shining leaves and the heaps of sunlit clouds that were the ruins of the vanquished monsoon were truly worth looking at; the postmaster was watching all this and was thinking, if there was someone with him now who was truly his own—at one with his heart, a human figure who was a tender object of love. Eventually he began to feel that the bird was expressing this same thing, over and over again, and the meaning of the rustling trees on this solitary afternoon submerged in shadows was also somewhat the same. Nobody believes it, and no one knows it, but in the heart of the meagre-salaried postmaster of this tiny village, in this deep stillness of afternoon, in the unending hours of a holiday, such emotions arise.

The postmaster sighed and called, 'Ratan.' Ratan was sitting under a guava tree and eating a raw guava; hearing her master's voice she immediately came running—panting, she said, 'Dadababu, did you call me?' The postmaster said, 'I will begin teaching you, little by little, how to read and write.' Having said this he spent the whole afternoon teaching Ratan the beginnings of the alphabet. And in this way, in a few days they had gone past compound letters.

There was no end to the rain in the month of Shravan. Canals, lakes and ponds filled with water. Day and night there was the croaking of frogs and the sound of the rain. It was almost impossible to walk on the roads of the village—one had to go to market in a boat.

One day it had been raining heavily since morning. The postmaster's student waited at the door for a long time but unlike other days she did not hear the usual call from her master and finally entered the room with her small bundle of books. She saw the postmaster lying on his bed—thinking that he must be resting she was about to leave the room. She suddenly heard, 'Ratan.' She turned back quickly and said, 'Dadababu, were you sleeping?' The postmaster said, in a weak voice, 'I don't feel well—put your hand on my forehead and check, will you?'

In this utter solitude of a foreign place, in heavy rain, the body, afflicted by illness, wants to be cared for. The memory of a mother's hand, gentle on his burning forehead, returns to him. In this deeply alien place, he wished for the loving, feminine presence of his mother or sister, and in this the migrant's desire did not remain unfulfilled. The little girl, Ratan, did not remain a little girl any more. At that moment she assumed the role of a mother, called a doctor, gave the postmaster his medicines on time, stayed awake all night at the head of the bed, cooked meals herself, and asked a hundred times, 'Tell me, Dadababu, are you feeling a little better?'

After many days the postmaster left the sickbed with a debilitated body; he thought, no more, I have to get a transfer out of this place. He wrote a letter to his employers in Calcutta referring to his illness as one he had contracted locally and applied for a transfer.

Freed from her duties of looking after a patient, Ratan once again took up her appropriate place outside the door. But she is not summoned as she used to be before. Sometimes she looks in and sees the postmaster absentmindedly sitting on the bench or lying on the bed. While Ratan is waiting expectantly to be called inside, the postmaster is anxiously waiting for a reply to his application. The little girl sat outside and went over her old lessons a hundred times. Her one anxiety was that she would confuse her compound letters the day she was called inside. In the end, after a week or so, she was called. With a swelling heart Ratan went inside the house and said, 'Dadababu, were you calling me?'

The postmaster said, 'Ratan, I am leaving tomorrow.'

Ratan: Where are you going, Dadababu?

Postmaster: I'm going home.

Ratan: When will you come back?

Postmaster: I won't be coming back.

Ratan didn't ask any more questions. The postmaster told her of his own accord that he had applied for a transfer, the application was turned down; so he was resigning and going home. For a long time neither spoke a word. The oil lamp burnt with a feeble flame and in one part of the room the rain fell drop by drop through the torn thatch onto a clay vessel below.

A little while later Ratan got up slowly and went to the kitchen to make rotis. It wasn't as quick as on other days. Many thoughts must have been rising in her mind. When the postmaster had finished his meal the little girl asked him, 'Dadababu, will you take me to your home?'

The postmaster laughed and said, 'How can I do that?' He didn't feel the need to explain why it was not possible.

The whole night, waking and dreaming, the little girl heard the postmaster's laughter—'How can I do that?'

The postmaster woke up in the morning and saw that the water for his bath was ready; in keeping with his Calcutta habits he bathed in water that had been brought for him in a bucket. For some reason the little girl had not been able to ask him when he was leaving; in case he needed the water at dawn Ratan had gone late at night to the river and brought back the water for his bath. As soon as the bath was finished Ratan was called. Ratan entered the room without a sound and, awaiting instructions, looked once, quietly, at her employer. The employer said, 'Ratan, I will tell the one who comes in my place, he will look after you as I did; you don't have to worry because I'm leaving.' There was no doubt that these words arose from an extremely loving and compassionate heart, but who can understand the heart of a woman? Ratan has for a long time quietly tolerated the employer's reprimands, but she could not bear these tender words. Overcome, she cried out, 'No, no, you don't have to tell anyone anything, I don't want to stay here.'

The postmaster had never seen Ratan behave like this, so he was taken by surprise.

The new postmaster arrived. Having explained everything to him, the old postmaster prepared to leave. While leaving he called Ratan and said, 'Ratan, I've never been able to give you anything. Now, while leaving, I'm giving you something, this will last you for some time.'

Keeping a little money for his journey, he took out the rest of the money he had received as his salary. At this Ratan fell to the ground and, embracing his feet, she said, 'Dadababu, I fall at your feet, I fall at your feet, you don't have to give me anything; I fall at your feet, no one has to worry about me'—saying this she hurriedly went away.

The ex-postmaster sighed, slung his bag on one arm, put his umbrella over his shoulder and, lifting his blue-and-white striped trunk onto the coolie's head, slowly walked towards the boat.

When he got on the boat and the boat had set sail, and the rain-swollen river appeared to be brimming on all sides like the earth's gathered tears, then the postmaster felt a great ache in his heart—the picture of an insignificant little village girl's sad face seemed to express an enormous, world-encompassing, unarticulated pain. Suddenly he felt a strong desire, 'Let me go back, let me take that world-abandoned orphan with me'—but the sails had caught the wind, the monsoon current was flowing swiftly, the village had been left behind and the cremation ghats could be seen on the riverbank—and in the wistful heart of the traveller being borne away on the river there arose this philosophy, there are so many separations in life, so many deaths, what is the point of returning? Who belongs to whom in this world?

But no philosophy arose in Ratan's mind. She only kept circling the building of the post office with tears in her eyes.

Perhaps there was a faint hope entering her heart, maybe Dadababu will come back—caught in that hope she could not go far away from here. Oh, the irrational human heart. Delusion does not dissolve, the lessons of reason take a long time to penetrate the mind, disbelieving even the strongest proof one embraces a false hope with both arms and holds it close to the heart, in the end it cuts the veins and bleeds the heart and flees, then one regains consciousness and the heart begins to long desperately for another delusion.